P9-AQH-225

PHALAINA

PHALAINA

Alice Brière-Haquet

Translated by Emma Ramadan

LQ
LEVINE QUERIDO
MONTCLAIR · AMSTERDAM · HOBOKEN

This is an Em Querido book
Published by Levine Querido

LQ

LEVINE QUERIDO

www.levinequerido.com · info@levinequerido.com
Levine Querido is distributed by Chronicle Books LLC

Originally published by Rouergue Jeunesse in France

Library of Congress Control Number: 2022931613
ISBN 978-1-64614-182-1
Printed and bound in China

Published September 2022
First printing

We discover a new species of life form every day.
But every day,
a species also disappears.

The fly has 8 chromosomes,
the hamster 22, the rat 42, the human 46,
the chimpanzee 48, the cow 60,
and the butterfly 380.

BOOK ONE

LITTLE GIRL

THE AUTUMN SUN SPREAD ITS last rays over the moss of the undergrowth. The trees gently swayed their branches, tracing downy dancing shadows on the ground. The leaves had turned gold and silver. From time to time, one of them would break off noiselessly and waft to the ground. Everything was calm, peaceful, and, besides the cadaver, which was already cool, the scene was idyllic. A few butterflies still lingered, flitting from flower to flower. The little girl followed them. Happy. Her steps were still hesitant, she hadn't been walking long, but she was enjoying her freedom. Barefoot, she weaved between the debris of the accident with that particular grace of young children defying the laws of gravity for the first time. Her little bouncing body, with her arms and thighs that had never known such effort, her plump cheeks, her fluffy cape that slid from her shoulders—everything seemed ready to cushion the fall. A paltry softness. Nearby a wrought-iron wheel towered with its spikes. A lacquered wood door laid ripped apart on the ground. And everywhere, the suitcases had scattered their loads of laundry and papers. The little girl advanced. The blindfold covering her eyes had come undone during the accident, and butterflies had appeared before her, minuscule and marvelous. They were far more interesting than that overturned cabriolet, more interesting than the strewn objects, more interesting than the shredded body. So, she followed them from flower to flower. How good it felt to walk!

"Little girl!"

Someone in the distance was calling to her. A serious voice, a pressing voice full of danger. The spell was broken and the child felt her legs tremble, her confidence pitch, ready to topple. Her large red eyes were already filling with tears. But the butterflies approached . . . Yes, they were coming to console her.

"Little giiirl!"

"Not so loud!" said a second voice. "You'll scare her."

"Little girl-little girl-little giiiirl!"

"She's not a chicken, you know."

The two voices squabbled, but the child wasn't listening anymore. The butterflies were there by the hundreds now, maybe by the thousands. The rhythmic beating of their wings filled the little girl with a familiar buzzing. With them, she was not afraid. They were her friends, she knew it. She felt it.

"Little girl! Come, you can't be out here on your own! It's freezing here at night."

"She doesn't understand you, she's a kid. Little girl, come here! Little girl, we have candy . . . Come here, you stinking brat, come on."

But the child was smiling. The butterflies were playing in her hair and tickling her. All together, they were spinning a web of delicate threads around her small body; it surrounded her, enveloped her, covered her up. The net tightened. She couldn't move anymore. Her breathing slowed. But not in a bad way. She had never felt so good. It was like a cocoon. The butterflies, gently, delicately, lifted the little girl from the ground.

The two men had entered the undergrowth and were gathering the scattered papers from all over. They threw these loose sheets into a large leather pouch, scribbled, crumpled, ripped, soaked, perfectly illegible. An absurd exercise, but the boss had insisted they leave not a single page behind. They weren't being paid to think, but to act, and on that front they were infallible. The bloodstains proliferated. At a distance lay the cadaver.

"Look, the professor!"

"He's in real bad shape . . ."

The two men were leaning over the inert, mangled body. The wounds were impressive. Truly.

The corpse was wearing a brand-new gray flannel suit and had a freshly trimmed chinstrap beard. Death seemed to be mocking this vanity of his. The face, so dignified, was stained with blood, and a pince-nez hung empty and useless on the torn jacket. And yet the body exuded a sense of serenity. Humphrey had dozed off under the effect of a powerful sedative. He hadn't had time to understand what was happening to him, hadn't had time to imagine what was in store for the little girl. He had departed in peace, happy.

That smile was bothersome. An insult to common sense. The sedative they had used to provoke the accident was normally undetectable, but, with the smattering of scientists the professor had for friends, they needed to be safe. Even a hint of suspicion and all the laboratories of the kingdom would set out in search of the truth.

"Better make the body disappear."

The two men got to work. They rolled up their sleeves and set about burying the professor's body. The task wasn't easy and took all their concentration. When they were finished, night had started to fall.

There was no more trace of the little girl.

They called out for her again, but the darkness complicated their search.

Oh well, they would say that she had died too. The wolves would take care of it for them. Last week, three slaughtered sheep had been found.

As confirmation, they heard a howl in the distance. Yes, they'd better get going. Too bad for the kid.

If they had been more attentive, surely they would have noticed the strange cocoon hanging from the chestnut tree, a monstrous fruit in the timid waltz of the first dead leaves. But how could they have imagined that such a small girl could end up so high in a tree? And if they had been told that she would spend the winter there, in a deep sleep verging on hibernation, they would have had a good laugh. Obviously, they had no idea who she was.

And so they left to take shelter from the cold.

UNDER THE LAMP

THE HEAT . . . the scorching heat that swells the thorax and lengthens the feet. That need to sprawl, to stretch, to breathe in the air and embrace the sky. He knew, he sensed that it was not yet time, but he couldn't take it anymore. Tensing his entire being, he attempted to break out of the waterproof coat that covered him. The effort required, after so many long weeks of fasting and sleeping, was inhuman.

All the better: he wasn't human, and everyone knew that butterflies were much stronger than those trembling giants of pale pink flesh.

So he pushed with all his might, spurred by this simple

certitude: for one hundred and forty million years, his ancestors had managed it. So he would too.

The membrane did indeed crack, and two wet wings appeared in the blinding brightness. Soon the rest of the body would follow: the head, the thorax, the abdomen. The insect would carefully unfold his wings, offering each of his minuscule scales to the gleam of light.

In this weather, it would take less than an hour to dry. And then: the good life! From flower to flower.

However, deep inside him, something wasn't right . . . There was a cog in the well-oiled machine of metamorphosis missing . . . He was willing to bet: it was still winter.

His new eyes couldn't compete with the crushing pressure of the light cast from above them, but he thought he glimpsed, in the back, a bit of bright gray sky. Fat flakes accumulated gradually on the window panes, which were covered in frost. No, he couldn't see them, and yet, he knew.

A shiver ran through him. The eye of light had come even closer. His wings were nearly dry, but he felt incapable of performing the slightest movement.

The lamp had hypnotized him.

He didn't see the needle approach his brand new body, but he felt it.

The cold metal pierced his meager body.

He tried hard to defend himself; his new wings beat the air frantically. But it was as useless as it was painful.

So he stopped and let himself be pinned to the board without too much difficulty.

Relief seemed to take an eternity . . . A vague memory came to his mind. A freshly cut field of wheat, its thick fragrance, its bronzed colors. Was it a real memory or simply a blurry dream inscribed deep in his genetic history? He couldn't have said, and to tell the truth he didn't care.

What he regretted was not having the time to leave descendants on the earth. After all, that was his reason for being. That was why the larva became a butterfly.

A painful hiccup shook him once or twice, and then nothing.

It was over.

John adjusted the needle slightly. The specimen annoyed him: there was a bit of wing that was still slightly crumpled, and it was ruining the lovely sequence of his butterfly collection.

Finally he unhooked the insect and threw it into the trash. No matter, he would force another to hatch. It didn't even put a dent in his smile. Life would be grand now that Professor Humphrey had disappeared. He turned out the lamp and cheerily left to find another chrysalis in the lab next door.

John was a perfectionist.

HUMPHREY

PROFESSOR HUMPHREY WAS AN ODD duck.

So, in town, they worried a little, but not too much. He would often disappear for long periods of time. He always ended up coming back, tired and with his suitcases full of treasures, fantastic herbariums and extraordinary stones. He would also bring back tons of writing: observations, impressions, thoughts, a whole flux of ideas in the form of letters whose addressees had a great deal of difficulty deciphering them. John, his right-hand man, had to clean them up first.

Hard work, that deciphering.

Professor Humphrey had always adored science, but hated school, and his handwriting was atrocious. The words were warped, tilted, tangled. And if only it was just that! Spelling was for him a game of chance, and he had a very personal relationship to grammar. For example, he believed that the period was a sign of distinction, that it gave a sense of importance. And so he used one after each word he deemed worthy. He found accents very gracious and added them as often as he could. The circumflex was his favorite.

On the other hand, Humphrey was horrified by verbs. In part because they had the nasty habit of constantly changing form, and also because he believed his mission as a scientist was to describe facts, not actions.

In sum, John's role, as his secretary, was difficult and essential. Hunched over his enormous desk, he would work diligently. Even if he chipped away at his hours of sleep, winter wouldn't last long enough to transcribe the letters from Humphrey's most recent trip. And yet he had to finish, and fast.

In addition, he also had to manage the Foundation. This too was no small feat. Especially with the ludicrous cold that had descended on the town.

The solaria of the Foundation contained the largest collection of rare plants in the country. They absolutely had to stay within an elevated temperature threshold. A botanical treasure trove was at stake. It was thus a continual source of stress: the employees were constantly rushing around, while anxious specialists came to keep an eye out each day for the first signs of wilting.

There were also the animals. Fortunately, there weren't as many now as before. The professor had decided one day that the relocation was too traumatic for them. He preferred to leave them in their natural environment to avoid uprooting them. Those that had been born in captivity had stayed there, though, and that was already quite a menagerie!

All this to say that everyone was quite busy and no one was worried. The professor would certainly return.

As for the little girl, no one knew of her existence. No one would have imagined that brilliant lunatic was saddled with a baby.

He hadn't wanted to uproot her either. But they hadn't left him the choice.

ALBERT

THE WINTER HAD BEEN COLD, really cold. Albert brought his goats to graze at the edge of the clearing, where the trees protected a few tufts of grass from the snow. That way, he could save a bit of hay. There were still some long weeks to go.

Albert knew winter well. He had endured it for more than thirty years. The appearance of the first snowdrop flowers didn't comfort him. That was supposed to be spring? Stupid flowers not even fit to eat. The first freeze would destroy their meager little stalks.

He advanced, and each step was torture. The humidity had once again made his bad hip seize up. He was limping more than usual, letting the snow seep into his old frayed wool socks. The wind rushed through his shoddy clogs and climbed up through his chest. He would fall ill, it was certain, his clothes were too thin. God it was cold!

Lost in his lamentations, Albert hadn't seen the goats stray from the path. When he noticed, he groaned and went off to find them. The animals had stopped in front of a bush; something was moving inside it.

What luck, a stray hare! Albert salivated at the thought . . . How long had it been since he'd eaten meat? Two weeks? A month? He grabbed a large rock. Longer perhaps? He advanced silently . . . Those idiot goats better not ruin everything!

The bush rustled more intensely. Albert held his breath and gently lifted the rock up above his head. He had to remain unnoticed. Another moment and the creature would emerge.

One . . . two . . . There it was!

Albert froze, he didn't know how—instinct, maybe, or luck, quite simply. A little kid had emerged. A little kid all scrawny and dressed in rags. She lowered her head, intimidated perhaps, or exhausted. Albert was hungry, but not so hungry as to become a cannibal!

"Whoa, kid, what are you doing here?"

The little girl didn't respond.

"Hey, little girl, do you hear me?"

Yes, she heard him, she slowly lifted her face to him, squinting her eyes in the white light of the sky. Would he understand?

"Okay then, cat got your tongue or what?"

No, this man wouldn't understand. He needed words and their strange modulations. She gave him a timid smile. That language was universal.

Albert took off what he used as a coat and wrapped the little girl in it. With his large coarse hand, he dusted the snow from her hair and removed the few dead leaves tangled in it. The child nestled against his chest, like a small animal.

"Don't worry, kid, I'm not so talkative either, I'll bring you home where it's warm, you'll see. It's no palace, but it's better than this glacial undergrowth."

On the branches of the bush, a chrysalis stirred slightly, then resumed its stillness, like a dead leaf. It was really far too cold to come out.

FIRST SPARK

THE CHILD WAS FROZEN, BUT somehow didn't seem to suffer from the cold. Albert settled her in near the fireplace.

Albert lived in a modest cabin in the forest. The layout was rudimentary and the furnishings provided the essentials: heating, feeding, sleeping, or, in other words, protection from cold, from hunger, and from intruders. The interior was gray and austere with nothing superfluous. However, several elements betrayed a woman's presence. Numerous cooking utensils, a delicately worn quilt on the bed, a couple posing in a yellowed photo.

Albert was in, fact, married. The lucky lady was named Bérengère. She was a shrew, firmly planted on her heavy legs and her fixed ideas, but he loved her. He was grateful to her for putting up with him, with his defective leg and his tendency to speak little and drink too much. Whiskey wasn't expensive and it was a way to fight back hunger in these impoverished times. Especially this winter. The worst one yet, without a doubt.

The little girl didn't move. She didn't even shiver. White, so white. She could have been mistaken for a marble statue if not for the regular breathing that lifted her shoulders. Even her hair seemed white . . . But it wasn't blonde, more like red . . . a very light red, sort of gray, almost faded. An ashen red, you could say. Its fineness was particularly extraordinary. Most of the time, it looked like it was made up of delicate threads of silk, but then the slightest gust of wind would come disrupt its severe straightness, and then it took on the appearance of a cloud of dust. Truly a strange child.

Albert observed her out of the corner of his eye as he carefully arranged the logs on the fire. He added a fistful of dried leaves and searched for his lighter, jammed in the fold of his pocket. There it was, he had it. In just a minute, the room would be lit up by the comfort of the flames.

The lighter spit out its sparks, and the little girl started to squirm.

A lacerating cry erupted as the fire consumed the leaves. The child, terrified, had curled up into a ball. Her squirming made her fall from her chair, and Albert watched her crawl furiously under the chest of drawers. He tried to grab her, but it was like she was possessed. He was afraid she would bite him.

Fortunately, the logs were wet and the blaze of the leaves was followed by a thin streak of gray smoke.

The little girl calmed down and curled up in Albert's arms like a frightened animal.

Terrified, she stared at him with her immense red eyes.

Yes, the little girl had red eyes—large, red, tender eyes.

BÉRENGÈRE

WHEN BÉRENGÈRE CAME HOME, SHE was shocked to find the house so cold.

The tall peasant undid her wool cape and snorted. It was freezing! She scanned the room with a bright blue eye. She was looking for her husband. The room was dark, but she knew it so well that she could instantly identify each of its shadows.

Albert had managed to put the little girl to sleep. Sitting in the moonlight, he had set about repairing the shoes awaiting him. Albert was a cobbler in his spare time. Or rather, when he had absolutely nothing to eat, he accepted work resewing, resoling, and polishing the shoes of a few acquaintances.

He hated this work. In fact, he hated the very idea of working. He himself wore clogs so as not to create any extra work for himself.

Bérengère insisted on wearing her pretty booties that clacked loudly across the cobbled town square. The primary function of those booties, perfectly maintained but extremely uncomfortable, was to infuriate her husband.

Quarreling was their preferred pastime. And Bérengère jumped at the occasion when he told her what had happened. She went pale and assumed her shrillest voice, her darkest eyes, performed two or three flourishes of the arms to give herself momentum, and entered into a complete rage.

She had stopped breaking plates, because of the expense, but she still enjoyed kicking chairs. It was better than nothing.

IT WOKE UP the little girl. Sitting in her improvised bed, immobile, she stared with her large eyes at the strange witch.

The sight of the little girl, far from halting Bérengère's rage, revived it.

Bérengère fostered a sort of hatred for everything to do with kids, tots, tykes, and other youngsters. She hadn't been able to have any and had thus decreed that they were perfectly useless domestic creatures because they didn't provide milk and couldn't be eaten.

A kid in their house? Out of the question! And on top of it mademoiselle was quite demanding, mademoiselle didn't want fire . . . Well then! For this tramp, they were expected to freeze the whole night? What was he thinking? He could go sleep somewhere else with his little wild child. She had worked all day, and she had the right to rest.

So Albert wrapped the little girl in a meager shawl and carried her to the goats. The stable was connected to the house. There, she would be warm. He would bring her to the orphanage at dawn.

He pushed open the door and headed to the back of the stable. Albert started to dig a nest in the fresh hay and set the child down inside it.

The goats, all at once, stood up and grouped around the little girl.

One of them offered her its teat full of warm milk. The child latched on and fell soundly asleep, savoring a sweetness she wouldn't experience again for many long years.

Dear Charles,

I hope you're well, along with your dear Emma, your adorable children and their adorable rugrats, and those earthworms you've become so passionate about. While you look out over your garden, I'm back on the open road. I'll still send my notes to you as always, but you'll have to wait a little while to receive them, and this time John won't be the only reason for the delay: there's no postal service here, no contact with civilization.

For many long years the two of us have traveled the four corners of the world . . . Our expedition on the Beagle *brought us, still young, to the most obscure countries of our surprising planet . . . And yet, my dear friend, it's in a forest here, a humble British forest, that I've discovered what night truly is. The immense trees, their dense branches keep me from catching a glimpse of a corner of sky or the point of a star. Impossible to know the place I find myself in. Shadow is everywhere, thick, opaque. I've been walking for a week and I feel like I'm constantly going in circles. Who said that the forest reverses the laws of reason, turns the knight into a savage and a straight line into a circle? I don't remember, but he was right.*

My reserves have run dry, but I don't suffer from hunger: there are acorns and there's water in this semiswamp. Life stirs all around me, and at times the night resounds with the creak of some insect or with the cry of a crow . . . Perhaps I should be worried about the bear I saw today, but as long as I stay at a good distance, it's unlikely he'll come looking for trouble with me. Animals are peaceful beings, it's only man who hunts for pleasure.

No, I am alone here, alone and forgotten by everyone, and that's a marvelous feeling.

Your friend H.

IN THE VILLAGE

TO TAKE IN A TRAMP! She'd already been breaking her back to gather enough to eat at home in their shack! It was true that he took on a lot of work, her husband . . . All day long, he foraged in the woods. She didn't deny it. But all the same, in this cold, to have one more mouth to feed when game was so rare! The creatures were hibernating, but the villagers' stomachs weren't.

Each day, the women gathered around a chimney to work together. It allowed them to save on wood, and in these miserable times, everything counted. Each of them would bring her little bundle of sticks or her log, and the chimney would become the living heart of the entire village, warm and palpitating, gently diffusing its heat to all those brave village women. They all settled in around it. Old Berthe in the front because of her gout.

Those who had brought their knitting would be in the front, where the light was consistent. The cross-stitch, and especially the stem stitch, didn't allow for any irregularity. Less meticulous tasks were spread on the sides. The farm girls, in the farthest corners, had to strain their ears to grasp the gossip that only came out in whispers.

But, more than the desire to save, what gathered them all, unconsciously, was the need to be together. It was the company that kept them warm.

All those women were much too proud to admit that they all needed each other. A naive spectator might think that they all detested each other: on the lookout for criticism, they were always nitpicking one another and went over the lives of their neighbors with a fine-tooth comb. But in reality, these trifles distracted them and gave rise to a tension that kept the village alive.

They needed to find something new in this corner where everything had already been said.

So, when something truly strange happened, obviously, it was a godsend!

Already Bérengère regretted having sent the little girl to the city. She would have preferred to entrust her to the vicar, it would have prolonged this adventure in which she found herself something of a heroine . . . Well, now that it was done, might as well milk it.

Louise, the butcher's wife, entered the warm room.

She had left her maid in charge of the shop. In any event, there was no one there, so she might as well knit by the fire. She took off her wet coat, grabbed a stool, and settled in next to old Berthe. Louise was an important woman in the village: well fed, rosy cheeked, her business gave her an important status.

This new listener was a boon for Bérengère.

She told her story for the twelfth time with a theatrical flair. How Albert had found the kid, her peculiar appearance, her bizarre reactions. Growls, shrieks . . .

Bérengère laid it on thick. Her audience was hanging on her every word. Louise had already stopped her knitting, the embroiderers were holding their needles in the air, old Berthe had stopped shivering . . .

Growls, shrieks, she scratched, she thrashed. According to her story, it was the kid who had refused to sleep inside. A real wild child. She had told her husband to bring her to the Sisters of Divine Mercy.

All the local institutions were discussed and the choice was unanimous. Divine Mercy was perfect. They couldn't dream of a better place to raise a little girl. Even Louise approved. She got her maids from there.

SNOW DAY

ABOUT AN HOUR EARLIER, THE snow had stopped.

All night the flakes had fallen, one by one, by the thousands.

Soon spring would resume its place, but for now, the forest doubled down on winter. She pulled her icy quilt over herself, seemingly in no rush to unveil her buds.

The carriage moved slowly. The little girl had fallen asleep on the bench beside him, curled up like a baby bird. Maybe she was waiting for the nice weather too? Instinctively, Albert pulled the covers back over the child.

A snap in the distance startled him.

He stopped, on the alert. His heart was racing. Where had that muffled fear come from? It wasn't like him—Albert wasn't the impressionable type. However, in that moment, he was faced with his old demons from when he was a child, looking for wood with his mother. He would stick close behind her and scrutinize the shadows dancing in the wind.

Unconsciously, his breath stopped so he could listen more carefully to that of the trees.

Another snap, closer. But this time the hunter recognized a small animal. It must be looking for something to snack on. He listened for another moment and could hear the soft, precise sound of a small rodent's teeth attacking the bark of a tree.

What was he hoping to find? The woods were empty at the end of this terrible winter.

Hunger was everywhere.

He had brought a little bit of bread but refused to touch it. Soon the little girl would wake up, and she would want to eat.

How peaceful she seemed.

He had a wild desire to squeeze her against him and run, run until they forgot where he came from. A voice inside him seemed to shout: *Leave! Leave! Don't look back! Leave! Your life is this way . . .*

But it was a crazy impulse, and he was not crazy.

He knew that Bérengère was right. They had a hard enough time being comfortable just the two of them, so with a kid . . . How would that work? Keep a little girl just to watch her starve, it was out of the question. At the orphanage, she would get what she needed: food and education. A present and a future.

A lazy winter sun was setting slowly at the edge of the woods, but its meager rays illuminated a thousand shimmers on the branches of the tall black pines.

Christmas had been so sad this year . . .

Yes, but hunger . . . hunger.

Dear Charles,

Weakness forces me to rest at the foot of a tree . . . Solitude and my frugal habits bring me to strange thoughts. Don't laugh, I feel like one of those hermits who in their extreme retreat think they're grasping the Truth. Incidentally, my beard has grown a great deal. Society, seen from here, takes on a completely different appearance. Our superfluous needs appear in all their absurd nudity. In nature, the struggle to survive is harsh, but each person manages with what they have without trying to starve their neighbor. The discoveries of modern science interrogate me. Your words on the origin of man of course, but also more political writings like those of Houzeau of Lehaie . . . What if the progress we are so proud of is actually proof of our failure? I'm not talking about all those formidable efforts that man takes to understand the world around him, and what we call science. Theory, always, is a beautiful thing. But in practice? What are we doing? We utilize it to conquer, enslave, destroy. We break everything we touch. The horror of slavery was recognized and the majority of enlightened nations finally abolished it . . . But this is not our only injustice: the worker in the mine, the child in the factory, the calf in the butcher's shop—each pays for our insatiable appetite. Up till now we have blamed the miseries of the world on a divine plan, superior and mysterious . . . It's time to take responsibility. Those thoughts flatten me at the foot of this tree much more than the slight fever I feel rising.

Your friend H.

CHAIN

In fact, Divine Mercy was closed that day. They had organized an outing in town for the benefit of the residents. Everyone had left. Albert had thus continued all the way to London, to the Sisters of Sainte Agnes. He had placed the child in the arms of a Sister who was very young and smiling slightly, and he had said, murmured, rather: "I found her in the forest, her name is Manon, she's afraid of fire, take care of her."

Then he had nearly run away to keep from crying. Manon . . . Why this name? He didn't really know . . . He had wanted to leave her with something, a memory of him, and this "Manon" seemed to him like a refusal, since he wasted each day of his life always saying "yes." He had thus offered this "no," and then he had left the heavy courtyard, trying in vain to reassure himself. There was no doubt, they would be able to take care of her. It was their job after all.

That's how he saved her life.

Because, on her way home, Louise the butcher's wife recounted the story of the little girl to her husband. Nearby, the delivery man was unloading freshly slaughtered sheep and suspending them from heavy hooks at the end of chains. The man was listening eagerly with his large bright red ears.

The delivery man incorporated Louise's story into his collection of daily news. He was a chatty fellow. He shared it all along his delivery route. From butcher shops to canteens, then on to the Humphrey Foundation where the two lions awaited him, perhaps his best clients, each of them gobbling down twenty-five kilos of meat two times per week.

He recounted his story there, confidently pushing the quarter of lamb to the center of the cage using a long stick. The beasts, not very interested in this easy prey, didn't bother to approach. He chatted while the lions lazily chewed the piece of meat.

John always liked to watch the large felines feast. A vestige of his childhood stubbornly brought him beside these great kings of the savannah. It was thus to him that the delivery man confided the story of the little devil, and the delivery man was pleasantly surprised to see the Foundation's second-in-command so interested in his chitchat. John asked him for every detail, made him retell a few parts, and even offered him a cigar.

This was because, the day before, John had in fact deciphered in the notes of his boss the story of a little girl. A little girl with red eyes.

John's own eye gleamed, his soul simmered. What if this little girl existed? What if she was alive? What if she was close by? All of those what-ifs made him dizzy.

He didn't have a minute to spare.

COMING BACK

ALBERT CAME BACK LATE. HE paced the sidewalk for a while before taking the road home, stopping at a few stalls. He normally avoided this kind of place, but today was no ordinary day: he needed to forget that he was at odds with himself. What he had just done vaguely disgusted him. It was stupid to say, but he had grown attached to that wild child. She was like a bear, similar to him.

He ordered a full cup of coffee, spiked with whiskey.

The night was cold, and he had a long way to go.

The alcohol was still burning his throat when he staggered into his carriage.

A little bear cub, yes. Maybe they could have kept her. The vicar could have taught her the alphabet. He himself could have taught her the names of the stars. Automatically, he lifted his nose. The sky was glimmering tonight. Tomorrow, no doubt, it would snow.

Drunkards make bad astronomers: nose in the air, he lost his balance. A vague nausea came over him.

It must have been that last cup, the one the owner had forced on him and which was heavy on the liquor. Whoa!

If he brought back the carriage dirty, Bérengère would give him hell for years. Out of safety, he lowered his nose, concentrated on his boots . . . his Sunday boots . . . He would have even taken his work seriously, if he'd had to take care of the kid. He conjured some slightly yellowed images from deep down in his memory. Souvenirs from when he was a young groom and he and Bérengère had plans for a baby, a bassinet, a rattle . . . But in the end, they couldn't do it. We can't always do what we want. And that kid was bizarre, after all.

Lost in his thoughts, Albert didn't notice the path going by.

The stars were shining.

The alcohol had dissipated; all that remained was the vague bitterness of his act.

He felt he had a perfectly cool head when he opened the door to his house. He even recognized the slightly abrasive scent of fresh meat. She had gone to the butcher; tomorrow they would have roast for dinner. Albert licked his chops and was particularly careful not to make any noise. Waking up Bérengère would expose him to a litany of reproaches. Very carefully, he lit a candle.

But Bérengère could not wake up. She would never wake up again.

The acrid odor of blood was not coming from a roast, but from that white neck he formerly so liked to kiss. The severed head was hanging awkwardly to the side. The mouth, cut from each cheek to the ears, opened onto a grotesque black hole in which horror itself emitted silent bursts of laughter. Her open eyes seemed to accuse Albert.

Terrified, Albert dropped the candlestick. The two torturers took advantage of the darkness to jump out from behind the door. They had been awaiting him.

Albert, however, was a hunter, and his tracking experience had sharpened his senses. His reflexes were keen as a razor.

He jumped out the window . . . and headed for the forest.

He ran over the frozen grass, hopping over obstacles. Now Albert regretted the whiskey, he regretted his bad hip, and many other things, for that matter.

He ran frantically, as fast as he could. He had to reach the forest. It was his only hope. He knew it like the back of his hand, the men would never find him there!

In fact, no one would find Albert. Ever.

But it was no matter to them. It was the little girl they were looking for.

BOOK TWO

IN THE SOUP

"MANON, EAT YOUR SOUP!"

No, truly, impossible. She turned her gaze away from the grayish liquid in which a floating round eye stared back at her. An egg. Every Sunday, it was protein soup at the orphanage, and every Sunday the scene played out the same way. Soon it would be seven years. Seven years that Manon had refused to eat her soup. The one time they had forced her, she had splattered their cassocks with a lovely gray-beige flecked with yellow.

"Manon, eat your soup!"

Why were they so persistent? It was stupid. But these nearly seven years of observation had led Manon to the conclusion that humans happily took pleasure in stupidity: their lives were stupid, their fears were stupid, even their dreams were stupid. A few figures took the place of values for them. Grades for the children, money for the parents, everyone was happy. Everyone could rank themselves and verify that they had more than their neighbor, or else envy him. This was the only force that motivated them, their true inner fire: pride. It was pride that, in this moment, made the nun shout. She wouldn't let a kid have the last word. Plain and simple. Stupid.

The nun's tone became more harsh. She was playing her part. Feigning patience. Every Sunday, the same rigamarole. They knew it, the two of them, everyone in the room.

Everyone was watching them. The room was immense, a bit dark, with long tables lined with endless rows of little girls. They all wore the same gray blouse. They were all equally stupid, or worked hard to become so. In seven years, Manon had never managed to make a friend.

Solitude or the vaults made the Sister's voice echo louder. Manon blocked her ears.

"Manon, eat your soup!"

Go on, get on with it. Manon took a deep breath and played the next part in the show: she shook her head no and closed her eyes to better imagine what came next.

The sister starts to get angry.

Her pursed lips tremble slightly.

Her eyes darken.

Her jaw contracts slightly.

Her nostrils spew smoke . . .

No, now Manon was exaggerating. Barely. But, if she's forced to be in the front row of a play, might as well liven it up a bit. Some Sundays, she imagined green scales, oozing boils, a dribble of drool.

Every Sunday it was the same, except in her head.

The Sister made the sign of the cross and grabbed the girl by the ear. Manon stood up and followed the nun, accompanied by that little barely audible nursery rhyme written by another orphan in her honor:

The larva goes to confess,
has the dinner of a princess,
her bum smacked with a baguette.

Larva . . . That vile name suited her well. A body that was too round, a little too pale, gestures that were too soft. Even her wispy hair had lost its gleam from being shut up inside. Her immense red eyes consumed by two enormous pupils couldn't stop fixating on everything she found surprising. Which is to say, nearly everything. Manon didn't understand the nun's anger, she didn't understand her fellow orphans' laughter, she didn't understand the superior's sermons. Wouldn't everything be so much simpler if everyone simply looked after themselves? Why waste all that vital energy?

Indeed, this world was a mystery to her . . .

ON THE LOOKOUT

HOW TO LURE HER?

At the Foundation, business was booming. Humphrey's death had been a boon for the recognition of the great scholar's work. They couldn't find enough honorable distinctions to give him. The mysterious circumstances of his disappearance reinforced his aura. He had likely died during a particularly dangerous research mission. They turned him into a martyr of science and cited his name at the start of every ceremony.

They impatiently awaited the publication of his most recent findings.

But John had no intention of releasing his treasure into the world!

The letters he had in his grasp were a real bombshell. And John wasn't the type to play around with rhetoric . . . The professor's discoveries went well beyond what that herd of scientific sheep could imagine. They challenged the very laws of nature. At least, the ones they had haphazardly tried to establish over the past centuries.

Yes, John wasn't afraid of big words: knowledge was standing at a threshold. There would be a before, and an after.

And he certainly meant to inscribe his own name on that beautiful revolution. He was already picturing the packed conferences, the prestigious universities that would invite him to speak; the students who would idolize him, rushing to his office.

He would put up a beautiful golden plaque announcing *Professor John*.

He would more than merit the title.

With a paternal gesture, he caressed the large leather folder containing the final letters. Humphrey hadn't had time to send them to his "dear Charles," and, in any event, since then, Darwin had died too. It made sense that John would be the one to profit off them, he to whom no one had ever signed a letter *Your friend H* but who had nevertheless been the companion in the shadows, he who had accompanied and assisted the success of his former boss, whom future generations would call his "mentor."

John crossed the room, went to the glass window. This large office had always been his, after all. The professor was always jaunting about and since opening day, John had managed the entirety of the Foundation. Humphrey had put up money, certainly, but without his loyal secretary it would never have lasted a year. It would have been a total disaster, and the wonderful discoveries would have been forever buried in their soft leather folders.

But now Humphrey was dead, and he, John, was alive.

He pressed his nose to the cold glass. He made designs in the condensation of his breath. Like when he was a child when he was bored.

He hated waiting.

The window had a view of the inside of the building. In particular, one could see the part open to the public. A group of students was visiting the Foundation's collections right now, under the supervision of uptight, strict teachers.

How to lure her?

To set the wheels in motion, he needed the little girl. Without her, the bomb would be more like a wet firecracker. They would take him for a fool. It was obvious. Yes, he needed her.

He had one great advantage: he was the only one who knew she existed.

He just had to be on the lookout.

Dear Charles,

Watched! I feel watched! What is happening? Am I going mad? For several days I've had a fever and terrible sweats. I'm trying to purge myself with roots, but I'm afraid it's only making things worse. The swamp water is poisoning me. I need to find a fresh water source. But how? I can barely even stand. I'm curled up inside a hollow trunk like an animal. I have to find the strength to leave. Here, no one will come looking for me. Except them. Those eyes, watching me. I think they're waiting for me to die. Vultures. I am reminded, Charles, how in the enthusiasm of your discoveries, you made us into big monkeys. Over our bowls of porridge, you explained our kinship with those large fruit-eaters, and how we had been perverted: we must have fed on cadavers during periods of great freeze, and the habit remained, became refined, was elevated to the rank of Culture. Thus the civilized man, against all logic, gorged himselfon the cadavers of beings that he had raised, sometimes loved. All of us, part of the same family . . . I don't know what these beings are, awaiting my death so they can feast, but in the end it's all coming full circle.

The strangeness of those fiery eyes makes me tremble despite myself, and at times the fever spurs a mystical crisis . . . Yes, I can confess to you, my friend, this childish feeling that these creatures waiting so impatiently are in fact demons.

Your friend H.

CRISIS

WHAT A HORRIBLE JOB!

Sister Angelique had felt a calling to become a nun. For as long as she could remember, she had always loved churches, those vast buildings full of shadows and mysteries, where the murmurs of prayers are heard here and there. The sermon was always humble and sure. She had felt good right away in those enclosed spaces, sheltered from the world's furor. That was where she could count on forming her future family. In putting herself at the service of the orphanage, she imagined herself surrounded by young girls. Lost, fearful. She would be able to restore their confidence. Sister Angelique let out a sigh. The image came back to her vividly. She had imagined herself listened to, loved by all those little lost souls that she would accompany on their path toward goodness.

If only! Laziness, hypocrisy, gluttony, maliciousness grew in those nasty little girls like weeds on abandoned land. And that one there was the worst of all. These perpetual Sunday scenes drove her mad. Why complicate things this way? Life could be so sweet and so simple.

That little girl, it had to be said, resembled the Devil. Her red eyes alone were enough to make the Father shiver . . . The fact that she didn't speak complicated things even further. They didn't know if she was really mute. Some thought she was simply stubborn, others that she was mentally disabled.

The nun grabbed the child by the ear and dragged her down the hallways of the Institute of the Daughters of Saint Agnes.

How long those hallways were! The convent formed a sort of large H over three floors. All the rear side, overlooking the garden, was occupied by the orphanage: the classrooms, the dorm, the cafeteria, but also the laundry and the kitchens. The west wing served the laypersons, notably the male servants. The east wing housed the religious. The Mother Superior lived all the way at the bottom. Near the street.

Manon docilely followed her torturer, bending her back a little to avoid her ear being yanked too hard. The pain didn't really affect her, but she didn't appreciate the discomfort of this forced limp. She observed the damp wallpaper and oriented herself by its stains and tears. Soon they would arrive at the portrait gallery, her favorite passageway. All those nuns painted in delicate glazing and looking like severe barn owls or grumpy pigs pleased her a great deal.

But Manon didn't have the chance, this time, to appreciate the view. Her spine gave way: a rip between the shoulder blades.

This pain was starting to become familiar to her. For several weeks now, it arrived without warning, forcing her to double over. Manon stopped, panting. Curled up. Clenched. As if to stifle the pain in the hollow of her navel.

Her body formed a perfect circle.

The nun let go of her and made the sign of the cross. That silent scream terrified her.

Sister Angelique, powerless, started to shout in her turn.

SILENCE

JOHN, ON THE LOOKOUT, WAS watching for the smallest clue. Never had he read so many newspapers.

In seven years of silent hunting, he had seen so many various sordid news items that several times he had nearly given up on humankind altogether. Drunk men in the river, women found in the gutter, children beaten to death, but nothing concerning *the child*. The newspapers were absolutely silent on what had happened to her.

Since the press gave him nothing, he tried another route. He spoke to the juvenile police force, building a few strategic relationships, notably with a certain Caravelle. A brainless snob whose greatest talent was whipping the air in arabesques with his cane, and displaying a surprising aplomb in his choice to wear ridiculous feathered caps. Even with him, John didn't dare ask the question that was burning his lips.

But he risked it one night. Over a game of cards and a copious meal. The maid served thick, perfumed liqueurs. The conversation turned to a couple tearing each other to pieces over a child: the little one had just disappeared, and the two families accused each other.

"One of them is obviously right," Detective Caravelle concluded, shrugging his shoulders, "and the other is lying fiendishly well! But which is which? Family affairs are the worst."

"You said it, friend! It's with our own kin that man is most cruel . . . This reminds me of a friend's case . . . if you'll allow me . . ."

Caravelle allowed, and helped himself to a big dose of cherry brandy and a slice of pudding. The next day, he would certainly regret it, but it wasn't every day that he had the chance to enjoy the delicacies of such a dinner. With what he earned . . .

"So, my friend is looking for a little orphan, but he doesn't know how to go about it. You see, that little girl was, how can I put this, born in an illegitimate manner: the two parents were married, but not to each other!"

"Ooh la la, a juicy story! Please, go on."

His eye gleamed slightly: the cherry brandy was excellent, and Caravelle loved vaudeville stories. The idea of the cuckold husband made him roar with laughter. He himself had never married.

"The wife managed to save appearances. Her husband, a member of the military, had been called for sufficiently long enough abroad for her to be able to give birth in secret. Only her cousin was aware, she's the one who brought the child to the orphanage. But my friend, since then, has become a widower. He has no children and wants to find that child again. A girl, apparently."

"He has to ask the mother . . ."

"She refuses to speak to him. She hasn't forgiven him for abandoning her."

"And the cousin?"

"Same, she accuses him of every wrongdoing on Earth. Female solidarity of the lowest kind."

"Blackmail? Threaten to reveal everything?"

"Impossible, the husband is a friend, double-crossed by an excellent duelist."

The police officer scratched his chin for a moment, accepted a small cigar, slipped a second into his pocket for the road, then shook his head. No, there was no other solution: he had to cast a net over all the orphanages and go fishing for information.

"If you give me the name of your friend, maybe I can help him out . . ."

John discreetly wiped a bead of sweat from his temple. Caravelle was a little too eager. Certainly, the detective was not the sharpest knife in the drawer, but detecting lies was his profession. If he started to suspect . . .

"That's very kind of you, dear friend, but it's better that I act as the go-between, if you don't mind."

"Of course, I understand your hesitation. You're a trustworthy friend."

The subject was far too slippery, his future was at risk, one word too many would be enough . . . Better to change the subject. John forced himself to smile and brought his lips to the minuscule glass of liqueur.

"You like our cherries? I'm delighted! Next time, I'll send you home with a bottle."

To the great frustration of Detective Caravelle, there would be no next time. A new idea was taking root in John's brain, a genius idea: an idea with zero risk that would be much more efficient.

ON THE ROOF

THE LITTLE GIRL'S SCREAM!

Lbn had heard, it was a cry of pain, no doubt about it, and it came from that old building in the shape of an H.

He grabbed the chimney-sweeping brush that served as his disguise and with a light, nearly aerial step, jumped toward the gray slate roof. His long legs, his immense arms, his narrow chest squeezed into his black vest traced large contorted shadows. It had rained a lot in the last few days and the roof shone like a mirror in the feeble autumn sun. It was slippery, but Lbn wasn't worried about the laws of gravity. He had finally received a signal from the little girl, and nothing would stop him from finding her. The edges of his feet leaned instinctively on the minuscule hooks attaching the slates. He climbed like a tightrope walker up to the edge of the roof and sat down for a moment.

The spectacle was gray, but grandiose. The shining roofs looked like the bellies of fish and the ensemble formed a succession of waves, transforming the entire city into an ocean of light. The desire to get a running start and plunge in those irregular eddies washed over him.

Impossible. Like every time before, the star-shaped wound behind his shoulder blade started to sting and a mute rage coursed through him, just a second, enough time to get a hold of himself again. He must not let the anger invade him. Never. Even if it was their fault, he couldn't lower himself to their miserable sentiments. Lbn closed his eyes and concentrated on the sounds around him. He had to understand where exactly the little girl was.

He heard the footsteps of horses in the street, the rustling of people busying themselves in their houses, the whirring of boiling kettles, the regular ticking of mechanical clocks, but no trace of the little girl. Nowhere to be found.

"It was too easy!"

His lip curled slightly and he clenched his fist. It was the second time his anger was rearing its head, he couldn't lose control. Absolutely not.

"No negativity. She's here. You just have to find her."

He had never been so close to his target. He closed his eyes harder, forgot the beating of his own heart and concentrated entirely on the sounds within the large building.

Near the east wing, he detected an abnormal agitation. Lbn felt it.

He took a running start over the edge of the roof, slid elegantly over the east wing, and wrapped himself along the gutter. The sounds were coming from the first floor. Lbn leaped to the guardrail and slid through it to peer through the window.

In their gray blouses and noses down, the group was entirely absorbed in what was happening on the ground. No one noticed the strange individual watching them from behind his round black glasses.

Dear Charles,

Fever devours me, I cling onto my sanity so as not to drown . . . It would be so simple to lose myself in the good old tales of our childhood and their superstitions. But if I must die, I want it to be in the name of science, and thus I record for you my final observations. I know that they will be in good hands. So here is the strange idea that came to me. This idea is to do with the works of Linnaeus—yes, yes, THE Linnaeus, the one who invented the nomenclature of species. I know, of course I know, that he's a man from the previous century and that your own works have largely surpassed his. You challenged the notion of race, and even those of species . . . But that's exactly it. I wonder if my strange little demons might be connected to those fanciful branches that we used to mock. Consider it, I beg of you. Linnaeus divides the Homo *branch into two categories:* Homo diurnus, *our branch, and* Homo nocturnus, *which he also called* Homo sylvestris, *the man of the forest. Traditionally the branch of great apes, but is that correct? As much as your* Origin of Species *largely demonstrated our relation to those cousins of evolution . . . Linneaus was a fixist, still bogged down in the prejudice that God had simply distributed essences:*

a cat is a cat, a man is a man, and each has his place in the lovely pyramid of the living. You exploded those naive certitudes. The world is so much more complex than that, and man and cats share a common ancestor, which might even have been a fish. So, what are these creatures I sense all around me? Men? Apes? Another species? Only one thing is sure: their red eyes gleam with intelligence.

Your friend H.

TRUTHS

A GROUP HAD FORMED AROUND MANON, who was still on the ground.

The young girls stared at her with some compassion, some wariness, and a great deal of curiosity. Manon was apart from their little world, and each among them would have been honored to receive a few scraps of her interest. Manon was so . . . carefree. Nothing seemed to affect her: neither the grades nor the reproaches, and those little girls who lived in the perpetual dread of what people thought of them would have given anything for a little bit of that superb superiority.

And Manon had a past. Strange stories circulated about her. There were murmurs that her father was a murderer, perhaps even Jack the Ripper! They spun extraordinary genealogies for her, the monster who falls in love with one of his victims and gives her a child . . . The Mother Superior, they said, collected macabre press clippings in a dossier to give to her when she was an adult. In fact, the man who had dropped off the little girl had fled, leaving behind him the cadaver of his spouse. All of that was a secret, of course, which meant that not only did everyone know, but also that each person added their two cents to it.

When the night was very black, to escape the boredom of the dorms, they turned Manon into a blood-guzzling monster . . . Because it was forbidden, all the orphanage had read the scandalous novel *Carmilla*, in which a young girl from a good family is seduced by the charm of a female vampire, so at night the girls inspected each other to be sure that they didn't have the fateful little red dots in the hollow of their neck. It was just for fun, they didn't really believe in it, but that obsession of refusing to eat on Sundays worried them: it wasn't Catholic. And to think that in a few months the little girl was supposed to have her first communion! The first Host . . . Nuns and boarders imagined frightening scenes each time: the chapel trembling, the altar crumbling, screams, tears of blood . . . They shook over it, they added to it, they laughed about it. Those fantastic images distracted them from the monotony of their days. The rivers of blood, especially, were a nice touch.

Gradually, Manon came back to herself. She was still on the ground, but the grimace of pain had been replaced by her usual indifference. Fear—like sarcasm—didn't seem to affect her. She was above that, or beneath it.

When the nurse finally arrived, she helped lift her up. She gently teased Sister Angelique, who had been wracked with emotion, handed her the little girl and dispersed the crowd.

With a gesture of her hand, Sister Angelique directed the young girl to walk ahead. She put a few feet of distance between them.

The truth would have disappointed them all . . . Manon refused the Sunday soup because she couldn't stand eating animal products. That was all. And since the Sunday soup was the one they added a chicken egg to, or the flesh of boiled veal, or the fat of pork slabs, or a bit of mutton, each Sunday the scene repeated itself.

At the very end of the hallway, the Sister stopped, adjusted her headdress, and solemnly knocked twice on the large door.

APPARITION

THE GRAY BLOUSES HAD SCATTERED, another gray blouse had stood up. No doubt about it: that was her.

They had managed to dim her light. A shadow hovered over her forehead, but the curve of her nose, the outline of her mouth couldn't lie: they were identical to the ones he saw in the reflection of the glass. Lbn felt a surge of joy, and his reflection cracked a smile. He wanted to pick the lock of the window to slide into the building and melt into the fold of curtains, but he was wearing that horrible canvas jacket that restricted his movement. These clothes were a barbaric invention, but a necessary evil to walk among these people without drawing too much attention. He settled for opening his large pupils a little wider. The little girl was walking down the hallway, he couldn't lose her.

As discreetly as possible, he followed her from window to window. Quivering from his discovery, he didn't notice the gardener walking out of the greenhouse. The man, on the other hand, noticed him immediately.

"Hey, Climbing Boy, are you crazy?! If you fall on my flowerbeds, I'm making you redo them!"

Lbn felt his soul snap in two. The Rule was the Rule: discretion above all else. Even if it cost him his life, or that of the little girl. How much time would it take for the guy to realize that no chimney sweep would be called on the day of the Lord? How many minutes, seconds before he gathered the whole convent and they called the police? In three leaps, Lbn passed behind the corner of the building, in three more he landed on the ground and found a hiding spot.

He waited for a few minutes in the trash area, curled up behind a large dumpster. Would the man sound the alarm?

He knew he was invincible against those clumsy humans, but he was much too afraid to raise any suspicion before he had his hands on the little girl. Now that he had found her, he had no intention of letting her go again.

The man's voice reached his hiding spot, followed immediately by the squeaking sound of his footsteps on the gravel. He was visibly out of breath, and his voice betrayed more worry than threat.

"Hey there, kid! Where'd ya go? You didn't fall, didya? Don't go dying on me now . . ."

But the voice was already fading. The gardener was walking away.

Lbn waited another hour or so. He needed to be sure. He came out only when he was sure that the gardener was gone.

Cautiously, he left the trash area and climbed once more to the first floor. He looked through all the windows, one after the other. Then he did the same on the second floor, then the third, went back to the first, searched the cellars and the roofs.

The little girl was nowhere to be found.

THE MOTHER SUPERIOR

THE DOOR OPENED, EMITTING A waxy odor of polished furniture. Manon took a large inhale and entered.

The room was immense, and superb, covered in green plants. The Mother Superior took care of them with zeal and the gleaming green leaves tumbled down from all sides. The windows were high, and the curtains, exquisitely thin, let the light shine through. It inundated the room and, besides the coolness imposed by the heavy stone walls, made one feel like you were entering a greenhouse.

The desk was at the very back. The Mother Superior stood there like a pretty flower. Her hair formed a kind of delicate corolla and her skirts blossomed naturally along her upright body. She was supple for her age and rose elegantly when the young Sister arrived.

That gentleness, however, was the result of an excellent education and required constant attention. On the inside, her heart was hard and cold.

In the background, Manon heard the voice of the Sister, who had resumed her litany. These tantrums again . . . Impossible to make her see reason! A nice egg soup, to regain her strength, we feed her too well . . . Such ingratitude! It was dreadful.

The Sister was exaggerating. She knew she would find a sympathetic ear with the Mother Superior. They had given up teaching the little girl morality: since she didn't speak, they had decided that she didn't understand. Like an animal. But now that the two of them were together, the moralizing lessons resumed with even greater intensity: one word bounced off another, the proverbs on a whirl and on a loop, preconceived truths echoed prepackaged thoughts.

In those moments, Manon let them at it and observed her surroundings.

All those plants. It was so pretty. The ensemble was tidy and organized. Blanchette, the Mother Superior's cat, was sleeping on the armchair. Piles of dossiers covered the walls, each nicely arranged in its cardboard folder.

A dossier for each little girl, a dossier for an entire life.

How many sordid stories were shut up in here? Several generations of abandoned little girls, tiny tramps left to their fate, usually dropped at the doors of the convent on a day of too much misery.

For these children's tragedies were also their parents' tragedies. Parents that were too young, too fragile, too poor. Daughter-mothers, sex workers. All those people who preferred to give up their child rather than watch them die of hunger.

A dossier for each little girl, a dossier for an entire life.

Those cardboard dossiers also contained a nice collection of mishaps . . . It was true, her fellow orphans didn't lack imagination on this front. Just last week, they had managed to switch the cassocks of Sister Rose and Sister Louise, the first being triple the size of the second! Sister Rose, furious, had gone out in a nightgown looking for those at fault, red with anger and bare-calved. How hard they had laughed! Another time, they put Sister Bernadette's underwear on the large wooden figure of Christ that decorated the chapel. The look on the priest's face when he walked in!

Too bad that, this time, it would end in the stick.

Manon knew the stick well. She was treated to it every Sunday.

Now the Mother Superior would take it out from her large armoire, she would tell the little girl to lean over the desk, she would bestow three stinging strikes on her thighs. It happened every Sunday, and it was better than eating the soup.

But no.

This time, something bizarre would happen. The Mother Superior would thank the Sister and tell her to go back to work. She was even a bit short. She wanted to speak with the little girl. Sister Angelique's mouth hung open and, in her confusion, she forgot to bow.

SNACK

A GOOD HUNTER IS ONE WHO knows where to cast his nets.

John came to understand that while speaking with the man who took care of his dear lions.

Luckily, the Foundation maintained numerous relationships with the different religious institutions in town, and benefited from their total confidence. Every year, the Foundation donated money at their charity events.

John encouraged Harriet Humphrey to invest even more on this front.

With her brother dead, it was up to her to maintain the family name. He organized for her a schedule worthy of a minister: tea with the Sisters of the Redeemed, a gala organized by the Community of the Benediction, an auction at the Saint Marie Institute. Each week had its share of social festivities.

Miss Humphrey adored it.

She got dressed up, dolled up, coiffed, made-up, perfumed, donned her most beautiful furs to go play the queen among the nuns and the destitute.

There, inevitably, people discussed the mores of the population, the decadence of the youth, the ingratitude of the poor . . . A family had once dared to complain of hunger, when they had just been given a new pair of shoes. Honestly! And that obsession with breeding children . . . revolting. Fortunately, the Sisters were there. There was never enough praise for these charitable associations. Bravely, these volunteers sacrificed their best years inculcating the fundamental values of modesty and decorum to the people. In those moments, Miss Humphrey was certain that she belonged to society's moral elite, and that sweet sentiment melded marvelously with the thousand and one flavors of banquets prepared by the greatest pastry chefs in town.

Thus, the elder lady Humphrey spent her afternoons complaining about human folly while stuffing her face with cream-filled cakes.

It was while biting into a delicious blueberry muffin that she heard talk of the little wild child with red eyes. She nearly choked with surprise, but managed all the same to swallow her bite with dignity.

With a few questions, she found out her age, her arrival date, and some information about the place. She made a superhuman effort to inscribe the orphanage's name in her brain, half-drowned in grease and sugar. The buffet had been particularly excellent that night.

She repeated the name until she got back to the Foundation, all along the way in the hackney carriage. She repeated it to herself walking up the large staircase, then revealed it triumphantly at the desk where John was attending to his papers:

"The little girl is at the Daughters of Saint Agnes."

CURTAIN

"MY CHILD . . ."

Manon was not used to such delicate manners. She raised her large astonished eyes to the old nun.

But the Mother Superior had stopped . . . Seized with a sudden suspicion, she went to open the door. The hallway was empty. She closed it again. Walking back, she deemed it a good idea to draw the curtains, and darkness invaded the room all at once.

All these precautions were unusual. Manon recoiled out of instinct.

Trotting in her little slippers, the Mother Superior resumed her place behind her desk. She struck a match, grabbed the chandelier, and lit a pair of candles. Manon gave a small uncontrollable twitch.

Hunched over her desk, the old woman read the dossier that was open in front of her. The gleam of the candles revealed all the severity of her face. Her nose was straight and dry. A beauty mark disturbed its symmetry and, from a certain angle, made it look like the gaping nose of a skull. Her tight bun gleamed with gold. Her neck seemed tense from the wait, and her eyes rifled through the haystack, searching for the needle, the thing that would hurt much more than the whip. Certainly this "my child" heralded nothing good.

Manon made an effort to peer past the flames . . . She wanted to see what the Mother Superior was reading. She thought she recognized a photo of herself . . . Her dossier? Her history!

"My child," resumed the Mother Superior, "I was going to summon you. I have good news. A man has come to reclaim you. A parent, it seems, in any case, a very good man. In a suit and tie. Very respectable. It seems that your life among us comes to an end today . . . I hope you will remember how generous we've been with you . . ."

The little girl, still glued to the wall, didn't seem to understand. The Mother Superior beckoned her to approach. Manon approached gingerly, skirting the flame.

The old nun pulled the little girl by the sleeve and whispered nearly in her ear, with a rancid odor of herbal tea:

"This man has asked for the utmost discretion. He will arrive by that hidden staircase any minute now accompanied by his wife. This was important to me. You understand, I would not leave you in the hands of only a man. We are mindful of our reputation at the Daughters of Saint Agnes. When your parents arrive, try to look happy. Show that we have taught you the best manners. I'll tell the others that you fled. You'll return to the world with your new identity. Useless to drag along the ghosts of a past that doesn't concern you any longer."

The Mother Superior talked, talked, talked, and Manon didn't know what to think.

She should have rejoiced, but a muted sound rang an alarm inside her, climbed up her legs, moved through her stomach, and resounded in her head. The ground seemed to be warning her, like when an earthquake is coming . . .

The ground? In reality, it was Blanchette, who was rubbing against her feet. The animal emitted a strange whistling, a hoarse purring that reverberated in the little girl as in an echo chamber. The sound became powerful, heavy. Her head was about to explode.

Finally, the door to the hidden staircase opened. The cat hissed and assumed a defensive stance. The Mother Superior also seemed surprised that there had been no knock.

Her face took on a look of horror when she realized that instead of the couple she had been anticipating, three men had just entered her chamber.

Three men! In her chamber!

She started to protest, but two of them threw themselves at her and forced her to keep quiet.

The third headed for the little girl. He was about to grab her arm when Blanchette jumped on him violently and tore at his face with large strikes of her claws. The man flung off the beast and sent her hurtling to the other side of the room, but when he turned around to snatch Manon, it was too late: the little girl had taken advantage of the commotion to slide between his legs.

Manon quickly grabbed her dossier and flew down the hidden staircase.

She found herself outside.

Free.

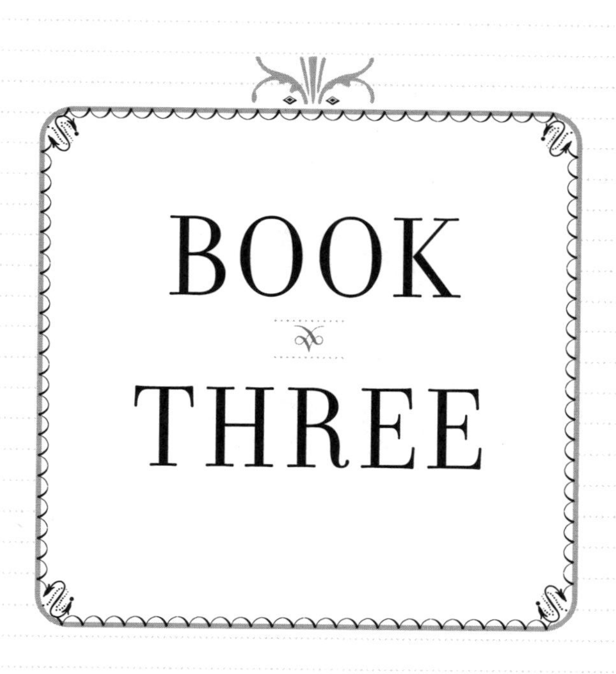

BOOK THREE

OUTSIDE

MANON RAN FOR A WHILE through the somber side streets of the neighborhood. It was the first time she had been so far from the orphanage. The first time she'd had to make decisions on her own. Make choices. Left or right. This way. That way. The infinity of possibilities had crushed her for a moment, but she had gotten a hold of herself: she had to fend off vertigo to keep moving. At first she had followed unending brick walls dotted with chain-link fences, so long that she had thought she was going in circles. Fighting back panic, she kept moving. The milky-gray sky had momentarily blazed with gold before turning to black, and the landscape had finally changed. The walls had disappeared, space had opened up, the street had given way to tiny wooden cabins surrounded by minuscule garden plots.

The odor emanating from the wet ground immediately calmed her. Her heart rate slowed, her step too. Manon wandered for a moment along fences made from old planks. In a corner was a stone basin full of rainwater. She plunged her hands into it with delight and splashed her face. In the square of black water, the first stars trembled. There was total silence. Night had fallen. She sat for a moment and reflected on the possibility of rolling herself into a ball there, in a thicket, and waiting . . . But waiting for what, exactly?

A snap wrested her from her revery. A voice. Wait for them to find her? Out of the question. She scurried off.

She concentrated on her hearing. Sounds were everywhere. Laughs, cries, music. She felt surrounded. Hunted. And terribly intrigued.

Where were those sounds coming from? A passerby? Young people? Children? For a moment she played with the idea of going to see, of blending into the crowd and tasting all this life that she had never experienced up till then except in books. But the risk was too great. She had sensed in all the fibers of her being that the three men who had shown up at the convent were accompanied by Death. And it wasn't the sweet Death that closes the eyes of those who have seen too much, but its cruel sister, the one that loves screams and pain. Blanchette the cat had seen it too, and her purr of alarm was unmistakable:

Run!

So Manon started to run again, with all her strength, drawing from all the unknown resources of her body. She shed her too-narrow shoes, which were hurting her, and felt like she was flying. Her bare feet hardly touched the cold, wet cobblestones.

She plunged once more into the labyrinth of the city. Its darkness, its bricks, its fumes had the effect on her of industrial muck and made her heave, but she felt, she knew, she knew it as though she had always known it, that it was in this grime she could hide herself from the men at her heels.

Like the insect that covers itself in its enemy's droppings to take on its scent.

And so Manon discovered her survival instinct. Those men were heavy and clumsy, she had speed and freedom: no one could guess where she would go because she herself had no idea!

GALA

HOW BAD THEY SMELLED!

Miss Humphrey plugged her nose as she moved through the crowd of the needy who were swarming the doors of the town house. They were there in clusters, women and children mainly, the brats in their worn rags, the others badly combed and with a displaced coquettishness, and everywhere hole-ridden smiles tried to cajole her. The worst were the kids, poorly dressed cherubs that already had that hereditary idiotic air, stupefied by the noise or by life itself, whose diapers testified to the hours of wait that their mothers had forced them to endure to be in the front row, right at the foot of the stairs, at the hour when the members of high society passed, so that they could collect one or two coins.

Miss Humphrey threw a few shillings at them in hopes they would leave. The odor wrested a hiccup from her. As though they didn't have soap to wash with. Cologne wasn't expensive! They didn't have to use Parisian perfume, either.

All those poor people revolted her. She expended great effort to get the most elite of her acquaintances to attend her charity galas, and here these people were begging at the entryway in their repulsive rags. They would scare away any important citizen with even a bit of sense and wealth. Truly, it was intolerable!

Once at the top of the stairs, she tried to reason with them. They were doing all this hard work for them after all. All the charity from tonight's big event would go to them. It would finance the vast distribution of Christmas brioche. The princess had even put her fan up for sale! They should be patient, good heavens, and grateful!

A voice muttered: "But we're hungry now." Another added: "Some bread . . . just some bread . . ." But already the young lady had turned on her heels. Her guests would arrive any minute. She had to make sure everything was in place. So she gave orders to the security guards to disperse the beggars, with as much courtesy as possible, and entered the luxurious palace through the revolving door without a glance behind her.

And so she did not see that Manon had just arrived.

THE HOUND

MANON HAD STOPPED, FASCINATED BY a strange spectacle. Opposite her teemed a colorful crowd. They were there in clusters, women and children mainly, the former strutting in their patched frocks, the latter decorated with faded ribbons and mended shawls, and everywhere embarrassed smiles trying to appear cheerful. The youngest, the kids wrapped up like presents, observed with their big surprised eyes this life that they had just discovered. Some were crying, frightened, and their mothers were trying to reassure them with swings of the hip and tender words, without taking their eyes off the staircase where the high society people were passing by.

Babies in their arms, older kids grabbing at their rumpled linen skirts, the mothers extended their hands, begged, but they seemed uniquely strong. Human rocks to which the toddlers clung on.

Manon smiled. How long had it been since she'd seen family? Had she ever seen it, in fact?

She squeezed her dossier against her chest. How loudly her heart was beating! She felt like she could hear it thumping against the cardboard folder.

Manon shivered. She was being watched. Who? Why? She didn't know. But a look, somewhere, had fixed on her, intense and black. Was it possible that someone had followed her?

She resumed her path, advancing at random through the streets, walking along walls once again, trying to pass unnoticed. A fine rain started to fall. She slid the dossier under her smock to protect it.

The rain seemed sweet. The silence calmed her. In the distance, the cry of a stray dog . . . Manon attached herself to this sound and tried to follow it. It was a thread in the immensity of the city.

A few passersby ran in the rain, but no one was paying any attention to her. They were all expected somewhere. They all had a place to go.

Manon, no. But she wasn't afraid, not of the cold nor of the night nor of solitude. Only those men scared her. She had to hide.

The cry was now echoed by another dog, an echo that was then doubled in its turn. A network was forming. She was certain of it.

Soon a dog came to rub against her legs, it was a long elegant setter. Then came a little basset hound, and a sort of spaniel . . .

Soon a hound arrived that demanded pets and seemed to want to guide her. Manon obliged, happy to find some unexpected company.

She followed them into a stairwell, onto boxes where they clearly had made their home. Heaving, she declined their offer to share an old, slightly moldy bone and fell asleep against their wet coats.

Dear Charles,

I think my strange spectators are trying to communicate with me . . . What a fascinating process, communication, and how many secret mechanisms are hidden behind a simple "Pass me the salt!" The person speaking must share the same code with his interlocutor, he needs a channel to transmit his message and a universe of references to decipher it. If I say something to you in Chinese, if I have no tongue, or if we are in the middle of playing tennis, the message will not be transmitted. But, similarly, a simple gesture can suffice! The language of animals fascinates us, as though it were a very ancient and slightly magical language. Scientists study the extraordinary colors of butterflies, the flight of bees, the song of whales . . . So many codes, channels, universes; so many barriers. But is that the real problem? Isn't it more that we don't have a desire to listen? It is obvious that the the pig whose throat is slit suffers and that the hunted deer is terrorized; a cry, a look, tells us this. Man has over other animals that superiority of articulated language, but it has rendered him deaf to the world around him. With his precious words, he has constructed towers of belief and myths and has forgotten simple reason.

We must abandon the mirages of language and find a way to face these beings that have now taken me for prey.

Your friend H.

MOLLY

MOLLY WAS A VERY TOLERANT woman who knew how to appreciate life's pleasures, but there were two things she couldn't stand: morons and rain.

Morons because without them the earth would run a lot more smoothly.

Rain because it made everything gray and damp and it scared off customers.

So Molly returned to her home in a bad mood that night. Was this some kind of joke? Two entire weeks of rain! How was she supposed to find enough money to eat?

In truth, the tiny vegetable garden that she kept in the courtyard of the building amply sufficed to feed her. She even distributed half of its yield. But all the same, she needed her real work! She couldn't be mistaken for a peasant.

Molly rolled up her dress with one hand. The streets were turning to swamps. The last thing she needed was to get dirty. With its three rows of frills, her skirt was already going to take ages to dry! And it was her work uniform, in a way. In her pretty pink dress, who would have recognized her? And who would come to give her money? Huh, who?

Molly returned to the courtyard grumbling, glanced at her artichokes, and went inside.

She was surprised not to find Giulio.

Whatever, it was his life. She was not the jealous type. Not at all. Out of the question to keep him locked up. Giulio could perfectly well sleep elsewhere if that was what he wanted.

Molly adjusted her pillow three or four times to get it into the perfect shape, curled up in her thick blanket that had been patched up countless times, and fell into a deep sleep.

A quarter of an hour later, Giulio heard his large mistress's snoring from the courtyard.

WAKING

MANON HAD ALWAYS SLEPT SOUNDLY and dreamlessly. Her nights were like short hibernations. It was hunger that woke her.

Manon ate little, very little, but often. Fasting for an entire day was torture for her.

The dogs had left, except for one, a big watchdog with gentle eyes. Manon stood up, dusted off her gray blouse. She had to find new clothes, and fast. Her dossier was lying among the boxes. She grabbed it. She wanted to find a place to read it in peace. Here, it was too dark.

It was a cellar, in fact. A ham hung from the ceiling. A morsel of dead pig. Manon shivered and looked away. There was a stash of potatoes in a corner. She took one. It was nice, soft and earthy. Manon bit into it with a satisfying crunch and chewed the tuber's firm flesh with relish. What a strange idea, cooking these marvels! The world was filled with bizarre practices that she had truly never managed to comprehend.

But she had to begin at the beginning: her history.

Manon walked outside with a timid step.

The light of day was blinding and Manon didn't grasp right away where the voice calling her had come from.

"Did mademoiselle sleep well?"

Manon's eyes slowly habituated to the light. The woman was dressed in a frock and was overturning the dirt of a tiny vegetable garden.

Her outfit was impressive, but Manon didn't know whether its voluminosity came from the woman's portliness or from the multitude of skirts . . . Both, probably.

The large woman approached the child. Manon, paralyzed, didn't dare move. The dog, however, was trusting and lay down at her feet with familiarity.

"So, my Giulio, this little girl is the reason you slept elsewhere? Well, we must bring her back home! Excuse him, mam'zelle; he must have been too afraid . . . You see, he gets yelled at when he brings back half-dead kittens or old stinking shoes . . ."

Her monologue could have gone on for a long time, but Molly noticed that the little girl was nearly folded over the documents she was holding.

"Are you all right, little girl? What brings you to Molly's house?"

Manon pointed at her throat hesitantly. She didn't speak. Not at all. And besides, what would she have said? What reason did she have for trusting that pink, noisy apparition? Shouldn't she run off again? She would have no problem escaping between the woman's legs . . . But then? As if in response, the dog came back over to her and licked her hand. She pet him, and through this gesture understood everything he was trying to tell her: Molly was a different human, she didn't care whether someone had a dirty muzzle or red eyes, she knew how to love without judgment, as animals love.

"No doubt about it, my dog has taken a fancy to you, kid. And he's a real watchdog, not a wimp like his old lady. He's taken a bite out of more than one guy who tried to give me trouble. Perhaps the young mademoiselle would like to come inside? There's water boiling; I can make you a tea. In this cold, it's not a bad idea."

It wasn't the woman's words, but the look in the dog's eyes that convinced Manon to enter into Molly's life.

Dear Charles,

Today the strange red eyes were accompanied by animals I had no problem identifying: beagles! An entire pack yipping in the forest night. Sometimes one of them breaks off and comes to sniff me before going back to its strange masters. If they've tamed the animal, then surely this is a civilized society. The presence of these hunting dogs should worry me, but my childish joy mixes with my scientist's interest, and I am both happy to meet these forever companions and fascinated to discover a primitive people here! We must notify our dear Morgan, who is very taken with anthropology and will soon study the Iroquois on the other side of the Atlantic!

Does this mean the dog is a universal friend? Guardian of the home, sheepdog, rescue dog, hunting dog . . . The dog renders so many services to man . . . But it's much more than that. The dog, in so many respects, is more human than man is. Your words will remain forever engraved in my memory: "The dog is the only being on Earth that loves you more than he loves himself. We've seen a dog in agony continue to nuzzle his master. And each person knows about the dog who, during his vivisection, licked the hand of the person performing the operation; that man, even if he made immense progress for science, even if he had a heart of stone, must have felt remorse for that act all his life."

That scientist was me, and that memory has in fact kept me up nights since.

Your friend H.

GRUESOME AWAKENING

THAT NIGHT AT THE ORPHANAGE was rather hectic.

The sound of the struggle lured the nuns, which made the three men flee. But the Mother Superior remained utterly shocked by the incident. She fainted several times and each time had to smell her salts. She felt betrayed: she had believed that the little girl would find the right path, but in fact she had given her nothing but trouble up till the end.

The old woman tirelessly brooded over her complaint, and each time she uttered the name of the little girl, the Sisters rapidly made the sign of the cross. No one knew exactly what had happened and that reinforced the aura around the old, ill lady.

Everyone got to work. They brought her a pillow, her prayer book, compresses.

Finally, late in the night, the Mother Superior managed to fall asleep. She was still clutching her favorite rosary. Her hands were tense, but her mind was relaxed. When she started to snore, the Sister on duty returned to her own bed on tiptoe.

She shouldn't have.

When the last candle was blown out, the men returned.

This time, they brought the old nun out of her convent and to a place where they would not be disturbed. The Whitechapel neighborhood had built itself a solid reputation for throat-slitting since Jack the Ripper had chosen a few victims there. No person with the slightest bit of sense would have thought to go walking there at night. It was exactly what they needed. In the shadow of the side streets, where a few destitute girls were obliged to work the sidewalk under the meager protection of woefully drunk pimps, no one noticed the strange procession. John entered a cellar, tied up the old nun there half-conscious, and handed her over to his men.

Their demand was simple: they wanted to know where the little girl had gone and who knew about her identity.

Her responses must not have satisfied them, for the interrogation was long, very long.

John stayed until the end and gave precise instructions for the staging of the body. The time period was rich in crazy criminals, and they were in the right place. They had to use their imaginations to measure up to reality.

When the men left the shadows of the cellar to blend back into those of the street, John nervously scratched his goatee. He tried unsuccessfully to calm himself: the old woman hadn't divulged names, and since the little girl had taken off with the letter and her dossier, she would soon reach the Foundation. No one knew. That was the most important thing. Now they just had to wait.

Wait, wait . . . And to think, he had almost had her! It was idiotic.

THE BODY

THE LAST DETECTIVE AVAILABLE IN the Whitechapel area was three months away from retirement. His mind was already in his little country house where he planned to retire as soon as he was free from his duties. Getting up in the morning, Detective Fagard thought of the fresh milk from the farm next door; walking around, he thought of the path through the undergrowth in summer; eating his meals, he thought of the tomatoes he would soon grow himself.

All this to say that he was in for a brutal awakening when he entered the small dark cellar and found the corpse. Here, there was no way to dream of mountains of potatoes that he would store for winter: everything exuded horror and cruelty.

The cadaver presented the modus operandi of the moment's current celebrity, the one all the newspapers were talking about: Jack the Ripper. Throat slit and stomach eviscerated had become a sort of classic crime motif. Fagard, however, had still not managed to get used to it. Just above, on the wall, large clumsy letters taunted him: a mocking, mud-colored *Hi, Boss*. He would send a sample to the lab, but of course it would be the victim's blood.

"They really take us for imbeciles . . ." Fagard muttered.

Other details betrayed the staging. Notably, they had removed the skin of the arms, hoping to pass it off as stylistic flair. But Fagard had a few years under his belt and knew that it was a skillful way of erasing any trace of an interrogation. They had also gone after the face. Behind the apparent madness of the gesture, the detective immediately noticed that no tooth had been spared . . . It was a methodical massacre by someone who didn't want the victim's identity to be discovered. This body seemed older than the usual prostitutes; it was probably an influential madam. In any event, she had been deliberately chosen and conscientiously erased. No, it was not the work of a madman, and this affair was likely just the tip of the iceberg of mafia muck.

Truly, this was terrible timing. So close to the end, Fagard had no desire to come into contact with humankind's filth. Their absurd cruelty sickened him. All of it reeked of a very time-consuming affair, and he had absolutely no desire to take on extra work.

In the end, he was there, he would do his job. It would be stupid to find himself with a professional demerit now. He took out his notebook, scribbled a few notes, and let the photographer do his work. The burnt smell of the magnesium lamp momentarily masked the odor of dead meat, which came back even stronger.

Fagard heaved. Seriously, it was time for him to retire.

He conducted a thorough inspection of the room in order to turn his attention away from the cadaver. It was a cellar like any of the dozen others in this working-class neighborhood. On the walls, graffiti attested that it sometimes served as a meeting place for the neighborhood thugs. He had to question the neighbors. In the four corners of the room were small clusters of white candles. Altar candles maybe, or maybe not. Those cheap little candles were extremely common in these corners of town where the use of electricity hadn't yet spread. But he would have to find out where they came from. And then find the name of the victim.

All of it discouraged him. Fagard scribbled another few lines of regulation gibberish and went back to the police station to file his report.

FUNERAL

WITH THE SUDDEN DISAPPEARANCE OF the Mother Superior, the Sisters of Saint Agnes had lost their guiding compass and didn't know what to do. Call the police, but the Church doesn't much like outsiders nosing around in its affairs . . . And the chaplain couldn't be reached!

Underlying tensions came to the surface. They had to decide on a successor. The eldest Sisters secretly coveted the empty desk of the Mother Superior, and the youngest started to rally behind one or another of the potential future queens.

It was great news for the young lodgers, who now received double the snacks without anyone realizing. Two days of remembrance and prayer were decreed, which meant the suspension of classes, and as much play as they wanted.

And so with few regrets and a great deal of delay, her disappearance was officially declared.

The chaplain had left them no choice. As soon as he came back, he lectured them bitterly. They had to sound the alarm and fast, mobilize all earthly forces to find that servant of heaven! They all nodded yes, insisting it was what they had been saying all along, but no one had wanted to listen.

It took some time to link the two events.

The cadaver was naked, without any distinguishing qualities. Given its age, they had naturally directed their search at brothel owners and mob wives. But soon, the medical examiner obliged them to change course. The victim had tiny particles of incense under her nails, incense that wasn't very common, used uniquely for night services, the kind only celebrated in convents these days.

The revelation was explosive and relayed under the seal of secrecy. They feared a wave of panic. If that Ripper monster was starting to nab his victims in respectable establishments, that meant no one was safe anymore.

So Fagard went through the dossiers alone, verifying the declarations of disappearances from religious congregations one by one. Mainly little girls who'd run away, young women deemed too turbulent, who had been put there against their will and who preferred to try their luck in the street rather than suffocate between those imposing walls of virtue. The case of the Mother Superior was very different and corresponded physically. They summoned a Sister to come identify the body. The beauty mark on the nose left no room for doubt. It was definitely her.

This break was a second stroke of bad luck for Fagard . . . A religious woman, and a high-ranking one at that! With a redeemed brothel owner, or even a vaguely devout worker, he could have hoped to close the case in a week tops, but now they would hold him accountable. There was no escaping it.

He brought the body back to the orphanage and took a few notes on what had happened.

He didn't even reproach the Sisters for having taken so long. At least he'd had two extra days to dream in peace of his future gardening exploits. Now, he would have to rummage through the manure of humanity.

The Mother Superior was rapidly buried in a private chapel so as not to let slip any information about the affair. But in the residence, the dark legend of Manon was brought into the realm of reality: Jack the Ripper had come back for his daughter to initiate her into the thousand and one horrors of his perverted ways.

POETICIZING

MOLLY WAS FAR FROM IMAGINING that her little lodger was fueling the sleepless nights of a neighborhood boarding school . . . To tell the truth, it suited Molly not to imagine anything at all. Imagination was her work, so when she came home, she enjoyed relaxing in reality.

Molly was a poetess. A public poetess.

She went to town squares to recite her verses and, probably to make her shut up, people gave her one or two coins.

Her frills, her ribbons, the makeup and all the bells and whistles were meant to attract her clientele: the passerby, the merchant, the sophisticated lady. Obviously.

But, coming home from these colorful walkabouts, the little girl calmed her.

She was always there, hunched over her papers. A studious girl, that was clear right away.

Molly, on the other hand, didn't know how to read. She had barely escaped the new laws making school mandatory and took great pity on the little brats subjected to it today . . . School benches, especially, seemed like a torture instrument. The people who had voted to keep children sitting all day had to be sadists.

In sum, Molly didn't know how to read, and had thus adopted the habit of learning everything by heart. She had the memory of an elephant. The hips and butt too, but that was another matter.

And it was easy to memorize poetry, since there were always rhymes everywhere. That helped. And she had started writing her own, too. It paid decently, it wasn't terribly painful work, and there was no risk of catching disease.

Manon didn't quite understand the nature of Molly's profession. She was often surprised to hear her benefactress rehearsing such lines as:

When the stars light up, don't forget, my petite,
Before going to sleep, you must brush your teeth!

Or else sometimes at the table . . .

Pass me the salt please, little daughter,
This insipid soup does not make my mouth water!

The little girl was often lulled to sleep by those funny verses . . .

Dear Charles,

This morning was, by far, the most marvelous awakening I've ever experienced. I'm not talking about the licks from the little beagle I told you about. That I could have done without, although that familiar presence immediately reassured me: to feel his drool, his slimy warmth, his rancid scent, means I am alive. I thought I was a goner. But then, the most wonderful miracle . . . A voice! And what a voice! Soft and limpid, light and smooth. The voice of an angel. I opened my eyes. A smile appeared before me, and two red eyes, the most tender red you can imagine. That of roses in spring, perhaps. Or of children's cheeks. Or of the moon, when the sun spills its light into the sieve of the earth . . . Paradise red. Not the Paradise of Sunday school, however: my earthly sufferings were certainly present! My throat was dry, my head felt squeezed in a burning vise, and above all, above all, I had a terrible need to urinate.

How was I supposed to explain all that to the beautiful angel serving as my caretaker? This is the kind of dilemma that people don't talk about enough in those chivalric novels.

Your friend H.

THE DOSSIER

HOW MUCH TIME DID MANON stay at the good lady's house? A month perhaps? The odious Sunday meal had stopped tolling the weekly bell and Manon had more or less lost count, carried away by the simple sweetness of savoring the moment.

The apartment was composed of a simple room that served simultaneously as bedroom, kitchen, and living room. Manon had insisted on sleeping on the ground, on Giulio's blanket. Molly had found that a little bizarre, but since she herself had a rather vague idea of "what was done" and "what wasn't done," she had eventually accepted it with a shrug of the shoulders. After all, if it made her happy, what did it matter?

The ensemble was simple, but sufficient. Bare walls, a bed, a little table, and a lot of light. The beginning of fall had been rainy, but the sun now shone with all its brilliance. Her life began to brighten . . .

The dossier contained several newspaper articles. Manon was finally putting facts to the rumors that had persecuted her forever. Notably, she learned that the very day when a man had brought her to the orphanage, they had found his wife murdered in her house and he himself had disappeared. They still didn't know if he was responsible for this horrific murder, or if he had been the unknown victim of it. Several articles contradicted themselves, responded to each other, added details, doubled down on the horrible and the grotesque.

It was clear the Mother Superior had composed this collection of clippings with patience and precision, inscribing on each little yellowed square the name of the newspaper as well as its date.

Finally, the dossier contained a more recent letter. A lovely letter with delicate handwriting. Manon inhaled the bitter odor of the ink. She adored that violet ink. It was a request for a meeting . . . The neat regular handwriting claimed to have new information identifying one of the residents of the orphanage.

In the envelope there was also another article, carefully cut out:

A GREAT NATURALIST'S FINAL ESCAPADE?

The evidence leaves no room for doubt: the car found crashed near the village of Greenfox is definitely that belonging to Professor Humphrey, who mysteriously vanished at the end of the fall. The famous naturalist was known for his unique genius,

often withdrawing from civilization to conduct research among the animals that so intrigued him. And so no one had worried about his absence until they happened to find the debris of his vehicle. No trace of a body, however. His sister, the rich Miss Humphrey, wants to keep hope alive and has called on multiple search operations, but it is very likely that the body was devoured by some wild animal. In this very cold winter, many such beasts have approached the villages in search of a bit of food. Among the vestiges of the accident, they also found a few effects belonging to a child, and there is speculation that the professor was perhaps accompanied. Miss Humphrey deems these suppositions absurd and libelous. However, the investigation remains open on this point as well.

Manon held her breath. An accident . . .

A child . . . Maybe . . .

Even more blood on her path . . .

Little by little, she was reconstructing the puzzle of her life, and she was no longer certain she wanted to see the full picture.

There was nothing pretty about what she was discovering.

Dear Charles,

I'm writing you something of a school-kid letter today . . . I don't know what to do, what to think. For the first time in my life, my scientific mind is completely useless to me. That girl. That angel. That butterfly, perhaps. Who is she? Of what breed, of what species? And do such notions still hold meaning? O Psyche, hybrid and splendid. Do you remember that ancient Greek myth? That mortal so beautiful that Cupid himself fell in love with her. He assumed the form of the wind to propose marriage to her: the beautiful woman would live in a castle with everything she could ever want, on the condition that she never try to find out his identity. At nightfall, he came to join her in their bed and Psyche spent many happy days in his invisible company. Until doubt started to sow itself in her mind: who was he, why did he have to hide himself this way? A monster, perhaps, preparing to devour her? One night, Psyche hid an oil lamp under her bed. Once certain that her husband was asleep, she lit the lamp to see him. Surprised by so much beauty, a bit of oil fell and burned the sleeping god. Cupid, mad with grief and disappointment, fled through the window. Psyche remained alone.

I don't know who is the god, who is the monster, and who is the lamp in my situation . . . but I know that, out of curiosity, sometimes the soul watches its happiness burn.

Your friend H.

AT THE RECTORY

AS HE DID AT EVERY equinox, Father Bertrand had taken out his collection of talismans and was polishing them patiently with a small soft rag dipped in a magic concoction passed down by his grandmother: oil, vinegar, and salt, a recipe that had the added advantage of also being vinaigrette. Sorcery is a branch of cooking, according to his mother, who was more gifted in pies than in potions. Father Bertrand, as he did each time he recalled his feminine role models, turned to greet the little familial altar he had installed near the chimney. A simple box decorated with tiny marble headstones, a candle, and a few fresh flowers. A tradition he had discovered during a trip to

Japan and subsequently adopted. Since then, each day, he saved a few scraps of his meal as an offering and made sure that the candle was always lit. So he was very surprised to find it now extinguished.

Something was about to happen.

A formidable gust of air suddenly invaded the room, knocked over the open spell book, carried off the loose sheets of paper, and rattled the amulets, which chimed as they clanged together. The door was open, and the candle relit once more.

BOOK FOUR

MALADROIT

MISS HUMPHREY STRETCHED OUT THROUGH her whole body and hesitated. Should she get up on her left foot or her right foot? She could never remember. It was terrible. And yet she prided herself on being obsessively superstitious. Left foot or right foot? It was the foot on which one shouldn't walk in poo . . . or vice versa, maybe? Gosh darn it, she couldn't remember. So she jumped at random onto the thick oriental rug by the side of her bed.

She would have much preferred for the first thing her toes touched in the morning to be the skin of one of those marvelous polar bears, or one of those two lions that did nothing and cost her insane amounts of money in fresh meat. When her brother was still around, he'd been so fiercely opposed to it that she didn't dare, not even now. The interdiction still hung in the air like a final wish. Too bad.

A capricious woman, she respected the caprices of others.

She slid into her swan-feather slippers—*Don't think about left or right, just don't think about it*—donned her voluptuous angora nightgown—*Don't think about it*—picked up her ivory comb, tidied her hair. Only then did she open the curtains of the immense windows that held back the stream of light. Autumn was wonderful.

She walked almost mechanically to the mirror for her daily inspection.

Had she aged during the night?

Yes, it was obvious. Again and always.

Her cheeks seemed a bit looser, her eyelids softer, her lips more wrinkled, her forehead more creased. It was dreadful. Every night she added to her ritual of creams, put this ointment here, that balm there, rubbed for a set number of minutes. She drank the teas with powerful herbs in precise dosages, boiled them for an exactly calculated length of time. What else was there for her to do?

Every morning taunted her with defeat.

The double chin especially revolted her. How many exercises had she done to make it disappear! But it was still there, quivering. There was no escaping it. A hereditary gift.

She could have cried with rage.

However, if she had looked more closely, she would have seen that her teeth were still pretty, white, and regular. She would have noticed that her eyes also retained the same brilliant gleam that heralded her teenage success. Her hair, especially, was superb: blonde, thick, cascading down her broad shoulders.

But no, it was the wrinkles and the creases that grabbed her full attention.

Perhaps she shouldn't have gotten up on her left foot . . .

PORTRAIT

FAR FROM THE NEW BLOOMSBURY neighborhood where Miss Humphrey was lamenting, Molly was pacing around the single little room of her apartment. Between the verses to memorize, the garden plot to tend, and the house to maintain, she was in constant movement.

Fortunately Manon never moved from the table or else there would have been a collision!

Molly was not interested in what her young tenant was reading. For starters, she didn't know how to read. Obviously. And also, she didn't want to be nosy. Manon gave her a hand with the cleaning. That amply sufficed. She wasn't going to ask for more. To each his life, to each his worries.

If you're hungry, say no more
I have a lovely meal in store!

Even so, she couldn't help herself, one day, from noticing a sketch in the dossier . . . A sketch that was not entirely unfamiliar to her . . .

It was the portrait of a visibly important man. He was well dressed. Top hat, elegant jacket. She was sure she had seen him somewhere before . . . But where?

Molly was proud of her memory.

She prided herself on never forgetting a face, and now this name that wouldn't come to her was poisoning her thoughts. The image spun around and around in her head. In vain. There was no question, she had to find out the identity of this handsome gentleman if she didn't want to go nuts. So Molly started to question the people she knew on the street, as is done in every good detective novel.

That was how Manon found herself saddled with a personal private detective, with questionable petticoats and outrageous makeup.

HANDOVER

FAGARD HAD CAUGHT WIND OF the strange stories about the little girl with red eyes. It was difficult to ignore the bloody testimonies of frightened nuns and the stream of anonymous letters.

For a time, he tried to gently stifle that path. A sadistic monster in the body of a little girl, it was a bit much, and the last thing he needed was the press getting involved.

But then he realized this was his ticket to being left in peace.

Finding lost little girls was the job of the juvenile police force!

They were thus solicited through their eminent representative, Detective Caravelle. This man was quite the character. As much as Fagard aspired to discretion, Caravelle saw it as a badge of honor never to go unnoticed. No matter the occasion, the man wore fedoras decorated with colorful feathers and proclaimed to anyone who would listen that he had never closed a case without identifying the responsible party.

It was true: as soon as an investigation became too risky, he passed it on to his subordinates, who muddled through it for him. Then he would add his signature once the case was closed. And if there was no break, well then, that was their problem!

Caravelle thus arrived at the convent with his current favorite, a certain Jalibert. The man was rather taciturn, scruffy and asymmetrical, slightly off-kilter, they said he was clever and ambitious. He didn't come off as very likable. He was like a discreet, tight-lipped crow.

The arrival of the handsome detective, however, had the effect of a peacock in a pigeon coop. They welcomed him ostentatiously, surrounding him with abundant attention. The Mother Superior's office was reserved entirely for him and one by one he received the nuns and boarders who believed they had something interesting to tell him.

No one had actually read Manon's dossier, but they had heard whispers of the macabre circumstances of her arrival. They recounted their tales with intense detail.

The descriptions were always more or less the same:

"Her red eyes, Detective! When you felt them on you . . ."

"And that deathly pallor. There was something unnatural about her, for sure."

"Every Sunday, she went into a trance! A furious rage."

"Blood fascinated her . . . As soon as she saw a wound, it overpowered her, she simply had to touch it!"

"Sometimes we caught her writing with her left hand!"

One of the nuns confessed that the day after the Mother Superior's disappearance, they had brought in an exorcist. Those priests specialized in driving out the Devil were rare. There was one per diocese, designated by the archbishop himself. They were privy to a few secret prayers that they recited when the occasion presented itself, and it was a way for the Church to weed out the authentic mystic-gibberish charlatans who abused the gullibility of peasants. Superstitions were high in the countryside, and people were ready to pay a high price for the fields to regain their former fertility or for their cow's milk to stop turning sour. Nothing very extreme. But Father Bertrand, assigned to the area, seemed to take his role a little too much to heart . . . The community was wary of this character and his spell book, and the Mother Superior had always been opposed to the idea of calling him. After her disappearance, though, things had changed . . . and that very night Father Bertrand had arrived in the convent.

Seated in an armchair off to the side, Jalibert observed the babbling of his boss and those women, sometimes noting a few words in his cheap notebook. Silent and unobtrusive, everyone had forgotten about him. When the round of thank-yous and condolences was finally over, Caravelle grabbed his feathered hat and headed for the exit without a word to his second-in-command.

Jalibert caught up to him, limping slightly. "We'll head over right away, boss?"

Taken by surprise, Caravelle stammered a yes, no, of course. Jalibert understood his boss's embarrassment and explained: "This Father Bertrand, we can't have him on the loose . . ."

Caravelle sighed inwardly. He had absolutely no desire to meet that sorcerer of the countryside. The meeting already reeked of boredom and dust. But he didn't dare say no. They couldn't have him on the loose . . .

FATHER BERTRAND

THE OLD MAN LIVED FAR from the town and its noise, in an ancient farmhouse covered in books from floor to ceiling. He was officially responsible for the twenty souls that comprised his minuscule parish. He gave mass for the three believers who regularly attended and baptized, married, or buried one or the other of them when the occasion arose.

But his life's main occupation was demons.

Over the years, he had constructed an impressive knowledge of the material, and people often traveled long distances to ask his advice.

He himself went running as soon as he heard rumblings of strange phenomena. Like a kid, he arrived with his heart racing, hoping to meet him—Him, the Devil, Lucifer, Beezlebub, Satan, Iblis, Mephistopheles, the Shadow Prince, Evil itself . . . He had dedicated his life to that delirious hunt.

Most often, it turned out to be an epidemic in a shepherd's flock, or an orchard eaten by parasites. Imagination ignited faster than reason, and people preferred to attribute the cause of their misfortune to some supernatural force rather than to simple bad luck. Father Bertrand then tried to reassure them, and if words didn't suffice, he performed a quick blessing. It couldn't hurt, and everyone was satisfied. On the other hand, he stubbornly refused to take payment. He didn't want any confusion: he was a priest, not a healer, and it was the Church's responsibility to meet his needs.

But he respected the work of healers. Over the course of his work, he had never met the Devil; he had, however, often rubbed shoulders with realities that were slightly different from those that were officially recognized, whether religious or scientific. He had on several occasions affirmed the efficacy of those sorcerers of the shadows and their knowledge, everything from magnetism to waves to plants.

He had himself amassed a respectable collection of herbs, flowers, and dried roots.

He took two pinches of powdered ginger, a clove, a few linden leaves, and threw it all into the simmering water. A lovely odor of herbal tea quickly spread through the small kitchen.

Father Bertrand poured two cups, added a spoonful of honey, and went back into the living room where his guest was waiting.

"Here, my boy, take this, it will replenish you."

His guest drank the scalding liquid in small sips.

"So, you found her?"

The guest nodded yes.

"And she's okay?"

Another nod of the chin.

"Marvelous."

The priest blew again on his tea and resolved to dip his own lips in.

In this tiny village, the tiniest noise could sound like a great fanfare. So their four ears perked up at once when the juvenile-police carriage entered the small courtyard. The priest paled slightly as he set down his cup.

"Lbn, get to the attic."

Dear Charles,

My God, my friend, where have I ended up? Who are these people? And the beautiful angel who has disappeared! I can't manage to get up, but my mind recovers little by little and what it discovers is appalling. No, these beings are not human . . . But don't get carried away, they are also not the primitive Quadrumana you call our ancestors! To tell the truth, there's nothing primitive about them. This is an extremely civilized society that has taken me prisoner.

Perhaps I exaggerate, I don't know. But my room looks just like a cage, and its entrance is permanently guarded. The walls seem spun by an enormous, delicate spider. Why did they save my life only to lock me away? Am I in a pantry? Are they trying to fatten me up? Their fiery eyes, especially, obsess me. And their voices, so lovely—I realized their words resound inside of my head: they don't move their lips!

And yet, and yet, despite everything, I don't really feel in danger. The hours pass by in a strange peacefulness, and although everything around me is unfamiliar, deep down, I have the sensation that I've come back home.

A trick of the devil? I've never believed in that nonsense but, goodness gracious, I would really like to know what that fearless Bertrand would have to say about all this!

Your friend H.

MEETING

THE AUTUMN SUN GAVE A very particular charm to the old rectory. It wasn't big, but still disproportionate for a man living alone. They could tell right away, from the state of the windows, that three quarters of the home were unused. The garden was also in a state of ruin. The elegant boxwood trees had become enormous bushes and the wildflowers had invaded the lawn. Only a corner of land was still maintained, a modest vegetable garden that someone had worked and mulched ahead of winter. Along the old gray stone wall, a pear tree spread its gnarled but sturdy branches, offering a stunted fruit here and there between two slightly yellowed leaves.

Caravelle and Jalibert got out of the car and crossed the small gravel courtyard. They stopped for a moment in front of the door. The abode, although decrepit, commanded respect . . . Was it ancient wisteria that ran above the door? Or was it that the wooden door had been warped by the years? Or else simply the strange profession practiced by the master of the grounds?

The two men weren't really of the impressionable type, but they both jumped when the door opened before they had knocked.

"Enter, please, I've been expecting you."

Father Bertrand was standing behind the door, a polite smile at the corners of his lips.

Detective Caravelle entered with two or three twirls of his ivory-handled cane. This gesture, which he had honed for a long time in front of his mirror as a young man, came to him spontaneously as soon as he entered a new and not necessarily friendly territory. He also smoothed his mustache with a measured gesture and made the tour of the room with a shamelessness meant to impress his superiority upon his interlocutor. He was mandated, he represented the Crown, and the priest had to understand this from the jump.

However, he could not completely hide his surprise. This wasn't really how he had imagined a sorcerer's lair. There were no spiderwebs, the house was clearly maintained with care and the numerous objects regularly dusted. There was no aroma of potions, the house smelled of wax and verbena. At a distance, a bread dough resting beneath its cloth gave off the acrid perfume of leaven. No impaled animals either; the man seemed more interested in collecting pious images. The images of Saint John the Baptist especially, accompanying Christ in his childhood games. An entire wall was covered with them and wood or bronze statues in his likeness decorated the mantlepiece. The furniture, for the most part very old, was chosen with taste, as well as the dishes and the tapestries. The leather-bound books were of an impressive quantity and quality.

The detective revised his judgment with another twirl of the cane and addressed his host with even more courtesy than he had planned:

"You were expecting us, Father?"

"Of course, a Mother Superior has gone missing, and my visit to the convent couldn't possibly escape your perceptiveness . . ."

"Indeed, that is why we've come. Could you please faithfully recount for us what took place during that visit? And don't worry about professional secrecy, we know how to be discreet . . ."

The detective sat down without awaiting an invitation. A knowing smile could be glimpsed in the curve of his thin mustache.

"I went mostly to reassure the worried souls. That is the quintessential part of our duty. But I can tell you what unfurled during my visit, I know I can count on the word of gentlemen like yourselves."

Father Bertrand invited Jalibert to sit down, too. He recounted for them how he had been called to the convent by the terrified nuns. He had scattered some holy water on the grounds and recited a few prayers, then left after a modest dinner. Nothing more, nothing less.

"The Sisters must have spoken to you about their suspicions concerning one of the residents. Can you please share your opinion of this story?"

Jalibert had opened his mouth for the first time, and Father Bertrand understood right away that it was Jalibert he had to be wary of.

"My opinion is dreadfully banal . . . I think she's a little girl mistreated by life, a child whose physical characteristics have caused her fellow residents to take a disliking to her."

"That's all?"

"That's all."

"The red eyes?"

"A case of albinism. It's clear. The absence of melanin causes a depigmentation of the eyes, the skin, and the hair."

"The seizures?"

"Epilepsy, intensified perhaps by a suggestive effect on the day of Sunday rest."

"That's a lot for a little girl, isn't it?"

"When you regularly frequent centers for sick children like I do, you see many such cases . . ." the priest replied with a faint, compassionate smile.

Yes, he was clever. But Jalibert insisted.

"Her attraction to blood?"

"A curiosity that affects many children."

"Her disappearance?"

"Ah, that, that's up to you to find the answer . . ."

Detective Caravelle slapped his thigh, laughing. "Ha ha ha, well said, Father! Excuse the impertinence of my assistant, he's a plain-speaking man who likes to economize his words. In any event, I am absolutely delighted that we are of the same opinion. This is a criminal matter, that's all there is to it, and whether the suspect has blue, green, or yellow eyes changes nothing."

The priest laughed too, and they exchanged a few pleasantries about how emotional young ladies can be. The two men took their leave of the old ecclesiastic and Jalibert helped Caravelle into the car.

"Boss, I forgot my notebook inside."

"What a scatterbrain you are, Jalibert! Hurry up, the nights are brisk in this season."

He wrapped his coat around his shoulders as he watched his assistant run in. His gait was lively, but lopsided and utterly lacking in grace.

This time Jalibert entered without knocking and grabbed the notebook he had purposely left on the armchair cushion.

The priest poked his head out through the kitchen door.

"Can I help you with something else?"

"Most likely, but I'll come back later, we've taken up too much of your time already tonight. Your tea is now completely cold and your guest must be growing impatient . . ."

Jalibert gestured at the two cups that had stopped steaming a while ago, gave a tip of his hat, and closed the door behind him.

The priest had been right. It was Jalibert he had to be seriously wary of.

THE SERVANT

NIGHT WAS STARTING TO FALL as Caravelle pulled into the station courtyard. Jalibert clearly had a lot of zeal . . . Caravelle had to make sure he didn't find himself in his subordinate's shadow.

Walking through the door, Caravelle understood immediately that something big had happened. The nun's murderer had just handed himself over to the police of his own free will. Caravelle let out a satisfied sigh. So much for all those extra hours, in the end the case had been promptly solved!

The man had been placed in a cell. Caravelle practically ran there. What he found didn't disappoint.

The suspect was an older man, in his fifties as least. He was skinny and gnarled, visibly deformed by a life of abstinence and obscure sacrifices. His hair was shaved, except for a thin and greasy gray lock that descended halfway down his back. He was wearing a cheap black cloth tunic knotted with a rope, a parody of the monastic uniform. His neck was encumbered with multiple collars, each adorned with a talisman or medal.

Caravelle glanced at the top of the file and knitted his brow.

"Your name is Xgyrtzwopl?"

"Yes, that's my name. My real name."

"I see. Tell me, please, what brings you here?"

"I've come to announce that She has returned and that the ritual you call murder is actually a birth, Her birth. Or rather, Her rebirth."

"The birth of the old nun? Of the kid? Speak clearly, please."

Caravelle's tone hardened with each word. He had no desire to waste his time.

"No, Her birth. There is always blood when there is a birth. And for Her, we needed sacred blood. The blood Jack offered wasn't sufficient. Poor impure blood, an insult . . . I had to take things into my own hands."

The man in black was driving him nuts. Caravelle wanted to make him spit out his explanations with a few strikes of his cane. He held back and, calling on every ounce of his patience, he said in an ingratiating voice:

"But who is She?"

"Our Mistress, the great Goddess! Some call her Lilith, Adam's rebellious wife, for others she is Diana, the goddess of the hunt, elsewhere they call her Kali, the goddess of death. Every society knows her, but none understand Her power!"

The man's pupils lit up, and Caravelle deemed it wise to bring in two of his men to keep an eye on him, just in case. He asked them to bring Manon's file—mystical flights of fancy made him dizzy, and he wanted to ground himself back in reality.

"So, you're a sort of midwife messenger?"

"That's right. I came to announce to the world that my Mistress has been reborn."

"And the mutilations . . . Can you give me some more detail?"

"The mutilations?"

"Yes, the mutilations. Tell me where the victim was mutilated and the reasoning behind it."

"Well . . . those are the ritual mutilations we perform on sacrificial victims while in states of superior consciousness. Our Mistress guides us."

The man was rubbing his neck, a sign that something was off, and Caravelle didn't need superior consciousness to figure that out. He walked around the room in a slow and measured step and took out his walnut wood pipe. The beast was not dangerous. The detective decided to deal the fatal blow.

"TELL ME, PLEASE, I'm really intrigued by one thing in particular . . . Why did you dress the victim up like a pink rabbit?"

The two guards nearly lost their composure, but a severe glance from Detective Caravelle kept them together. They assumed their most sinister expressions. The man seemed distraught . . . Obviously he hadn't been expecting this question and his source hadn't been solid enough for him to be able to contradict the police. He felt trapped.

"I . . . I . . . I refuse to divulge the magical rituals of our ceremonies! That is information that only the initiated are privy to."

The man then shut down in a stubborn silence, but Caravelle didn't mind—he had gotten his answer. This was a madman, nothing more.

The advantage of all this was that he could have an early dinner. But as he sat down at the table, he thought to himself that it was really a shame . . . Nothing goes better with a meal than the closing of a case. He would console himself with an excellent bottle of wine.

LBN

FATHER BERTRAND EMPTIED THE CUPS in the sink and rinsed them with warm water. As he was doing so, he knocked on the pipe three times. It was the signal, but Lbn, who hadn't missed any of the conversation, was already on the move. He was fleeing for his life, for his survival. He snaked through the chimney and climbed with agility. A small roof protected the foyer from the rain and offered him an excellent observation post. It took him a few seconds to locate Jalibert, hidden behind the row of linden trees.

The gentleman had lit a fire and was waiting for the duck to come out. He had found an excuse to exit the car and ditch his joke of a boss. He was clever, but he didn't know that he was going after an organization that exceeded his wildest imagination.

The rectory was constructed on a complex network of tunnels that had formerly served as military defenses.

Lbn greeted Father Bertrand, then slid down to the cellar, taking the vents. One could never be too careful. He jumped without hesitation into the immense heap of charcoal. He knew how to find the trap all the way at the bottom right, the one that opened onto the extraordinary labyrinth of underground passageways. It was all simply a matter of orientation. The paths were countless, and each fork was a new occasion for the mere mortal to get lost.

But Lbn was no mere mortal. He passed beneath the row of linden trees. He stopped for a moment, his nose lifted toward their roots. Jalibert must have been just above him. He concentrated and tried to capture the vibrations of this new enemy.

The two meters of earth probably muted his sensations, but he didn't feel the aggression he expected. It was mainly curiosity that seemed to motivate Detective Jalibert. Curiosity, solitude, and something else . . .

Realizing that it was hope emanating from this man above him, Lbn furrowed his funny brow. If he'd had the time, he would have liked to know more about this strange policeman. But he had to find the little girl. Since her arrival at Molly's house, he had kept constant watch over her—with the help of Giulio, of course. He had left her for a moment to update Father Bertrand, but now he understood the risk: He wasn't the only one searching for her . . . How naive he had been!

He had to get her far away from here, and fast.

JALIBERT

JALIBERT WAITED UNDER THE LINDEN tree for an hour, then two, then three. He was sure he would see the mysterious guest leave, and just as sure that this person, whoever it was, would bring him right to the little girl.

But the hours passed and Jalibert soon had to resign himself to spending the night at his observation post. It wasn't until the early morning, when the living room was lit again, that he lost all hope and went to knock on the door, resolved to search the rectory if necessary.

The priest once again opened with a "Come in, I've been expecting you" that Jalibert received with much less composure than the first time. You can't strike a man of the Church, of course, but you could give him a little nudge. Jalibert wanted him to pay for his night under the linden tree at the very least.

But the old man remained completely impassive to the policeman's curtness.

"Would you like an herbal tea?"

"Hmmm . . . I was told not to drink the potions of sorcerers."

"You have sharp judgment, my boy. But who told you I was one of them?"

"A little birdie . . ."

"Rumors then. The same rumors that turned that little girl into the daughter of a monster. So, I'll ask you again, would you like an herbal tea? With some toast? I have elderberry jam, and I make the bread myself with a natural leaven that's several centuries old."

Jalibert yielded to the floral fragrance of the breakfast: the herbal tea was delicious, the jam exquisite, and it's hard to think clearly on an empty stomach. He needed all his wits about him. The old priest was seductive; he knew how to sugarcoat things and turn them to his advantage. It was hard to stand up to him: he unraveled the arguments of his opposition, and you soon found yourself in agreement with him without even realizing it.

Jalibert, tired from his sleepless night, had to make a violent effort to resist his game.

"So, this guest of yours? I'd bet my shirt he's no longer in the house. Did he evaporate?"

"Keep your shirt then, young man, the servants of the Lord don't have that kind of pizzazz."

"So he flew away?"

"You would have seen him, the view is excellent from the path of linden trees."

Don't get aggravated, don't get aggravated. Raising a hand to a priest could cost you. Breathe, blow on the tea, bite into the toast, chew, swallow, and begin again.

"Let's speak candidly, Father. My intentions are good, approved by your Lord and all that jazz, I swear on the Bible or on whatever you like. I have to find that little girl. I'm certain you know much more than you want me to think, and your guest, since he hid at our arrival, must also have some key information."

"It could have been a parishioner trying to be discreet."

"It could have been, but it wasn't. Father, I'm asking you, please stop taking us for imbeciles, we're losing time."

"No, my son, we're gaining time. You seem like someone intelligent, and your intentions do in fact seem to follow noble sentiments. But you are dogged by a sin, the worst sin of all . . ."

"Which one, Father?"

"Pride, young man, pride. Who are you to deem your enterprise 'good'? In this matter, the only path of wisdom is that of ignorance. Believe me, my son, it's in the name of Goodness that I will tell you nothing, absolutely nothing, not even under torture."

The priest was a skillful debater and incredibly stubborn; Jalibert knew he would get nothing out of him. He was seething, but anger wouldn't help him this time. Violence—like patience—wouldn't suffice. He needed to use his intelligence. So he stood up and headed for the door.

"Thank you, Father, for this delicious breakfast."

"Goodbye, my son, and heed my advice: if your intentions are good, truly good, stop searching for her."

ARCHIVES

JALIBERT DIDN'T HAVE A CHOICE, he had to return to the source. So he asked the legal authorities if he could go through the archives in the little village where they had found the child.

He and his giant mustache entered the local station's basement. It was dark and dusty and there were files everywhere. How could such a tranquil hamlet accumulate so much paperwork? It was one of the great mysteries of public service.

The archives bore witness to the strange accident. The disappearances.

The official report did in fact mention the presence of children's clothing found in the debris of the cabriolet. Jalibert rifled through the newspapers from the time. They had all recounted the tragedy in some capacity. Professor Humphrey was an important person because of his work, but also because of his wealth, and his disappearance had been highly publicized. A martyr for science—a good story for a paper, no doubt about it.

None, however, had given much attention to the possible presence of a child . . . Miss Humphrey, the grieving sister, must have hushed up the affair before she became the target of a scandal. Jalibert had seen that kind of thing before. It was pretty simple when you had a padded wallet. It seemed no one had looked into it . . .

Could that have been Manon? The dates didn't sit right with Jalibert. Several months separated the time of the accident from the discovery of the wild child. The winter had been particularly brutal that year. He had experienced it firsthand . . . How could such a young child have survived alone in that icy wilderness?

But it wasn't impossible.

What was her connection to what had happened? Bérengère's murder was also related; the local newspaper seemed to accuse the husband who'd fled. They suspected him of taking off with the child after killing his wife in a fit of madness. The newspaper called on the testimony of Louise, the butcher's wife. The victim had confessed her anxieties to Louise not long before she'd died. Apparently she didn't feel safe in her home anymore. The butcher's wife digressed, expressed concern for the village, for business. Apparently the nation's economy was at risk.

Jalibert crumpled the paper despite himself. It wasn't very professional, but this heap of absurdity was unbearable to him.

No matter. There were too many accidents linked to the little girl for it to be a coincidence. But her role was difficult to define: Was she the cause or the consequence of it all? Guilty or victim? He didn't know.

Society links childhood to the notion of innocence, but in reality childhood is a moment of unconsciousness: the norms of society have not yet hindered our freedom, and children act on their primal instincts. They are without malice, but without goodness either, and can commit the worst cruelties with no ulterior motive.

Had the child provoked these accidents?

He had to go even further back. To the little girl's origins. To the great professor's final months. To his story. To his notes.

Their absence electrified him.

A professor takes notes, don't they? People like that are always writing . . . Yet Jalibert had read and reread the documents, and there hadn't been any mention of them. Clothing, instruments, a few small tools, samples of plants and minerals . . . and not a single piece of paper or notebook? No one had found that strange at the time?

Either the professor had hidden his notes before he died, or someone had taken them from him. In any case, Jalibert had to get his hands on them.

The hunt was on.

BOOK FIVE

TO THE COUNTRYSIDE

MISS HUMPHREY WAS EATING SLOWLY, in little mouthfuls that she chewed for a long time, as her physiologist friend had advised her. She took a third helping of the roast. She'd had a dizzy spell that very morning and her personal doctor had told her not to skimp on protein. She then downed two large glasses of thick, sweet wine, as her surgeon had recommended, and finished the meal with a packet of honey candies, recommended by an herbalist she knew who claimed it was an excellent preventative treatment for a range of illnesses.

You should always listen to doctors.

John was incredibly stubborn, he called all this advice idiocy. He had completed medical school too, yes, but he had specialized in veterinary medicine, so to each his work. Let him stick to collecting centipedes.

On that note, had anyone ever seen a centipede in good health? Huh?

Miss Humphrey opened another packet of honey candy.

The truth was that she adored honey candy. And wine, and meat, for that matter.

Oddly, John wasn't taking more helpings tonight. He seemed preoccupied.

She shoved three more candies into her mouth, which she swallowed whole before asking about her lover's gloomy mood.

"Darling, is something wrong?"

Nose in his plate, he was poking his untouched roast with the end of his fork. He didn't answer, lost in thought.

"Daaaaarling! Is something wrong?"

He lifted his nose this time, but his expression was so sullen that she was sorry to have insisted. Apparently something was wrong, seriously wrong, and under no circumstances could she be vexed during the first phase of digestion, or she was sure to have heart palpitations. Her hygienist had told her that.

John gathered himself and carefully folded his table napkin.

"Sweetheart, pack your bags, we're going away for a few days."

Not such bad news after all!

Dear Charles,

I described myself as prey in my last letter, but today I am the most spoiled guest! It would perhaps be an exaggeration to speak of friendship, but I have at least earned their trust. It happened in the strangest way.

I was still recovering, sprawled in my spiderweb bed, when suddenly I heard a terrible racket. It was so unexpected in this world of cotton that I found the strength to get up and see what was happening. One of them had been wounded: a child had been struck in the shoulder by a blazing arrow. Everyone was looking at him without moving, as though stupefied by the horror of the situation. Out of reflex, I took off what remained of my jacket and put out the fire threatening the tiny being. Their eyes slowly came back to life. I laid the child down to try to remove the steel arrow, but calm had already returned. They were all smiling, even the little wounded child.

They brought me back to my room. Two hours later, the child brought me fruit as a sign of gratitude, and who accompanied him? The beautiful angel! The resemblance was striking. His sister, no doubt, or in any case a relative.

The child, contrary to all laws of medicine, was perfectly healed. Only a small star-shaped scar on his shoulder assured me that I hadn't dreamed it all.

Since then, everyone has been perfectly kind to me and life is exquisitely sweet. No, I don't think I'll go back to the city.

Your friend H.

GROUND

OF COURSE, THE FOREST HAD stifled its secret for a long time. There remained no trace of the accident that had taken place nearly eight years prior . . . But the inhabitants of the village on the other side of the woods remembered. Walking up the path, Jalibert found witnesses confirming that the professor had been accompanied by a child. He even found a small inn near the main town where they had stayed. The owner was unequivocal.

"Of course I remember! That smartly dressed gentleman and his funny kid . . . It was cold that winter, so cold . . . It was crazy to travel with such a young child. It took us years to travel with my

Big Jack, just imagine that kid in the glacial torrents. Of course, that made my stomach churn, or my instinct, anyway, you get it."

The inn keeper wiped a rag over the large oak table. Jalibert lifted his mug of foamy beer; he was ecstatic. It was all coming together. He just had to keep digging.

"Madam, I'm going to ask you to strain your memory, but it's important. It was a long time ago, I'm well aware, but please, tell me: Did you notice anything bizarre?"

The large woman burst into laughter fit for an ogress and launched a few yellowish wads of spit onto the table she had just wiped. Jalibert pushed his mug away with a disgusted grimace.

"Anything bizarre? Everything about them was bizarre! For starters, the man didn't talk like everyone else, he jabbered on in a funny gobbledygook that you could understand a few words of but not all. And then the kid, ah, that kid! She had a big bandage around the eyes, a black one, supposedly she'd just been operated on, but it looked as much like a hospital bandage as my behind looks like a violin!"

She accompanied this affirmation with a nice smack on her round rump before continuing.

"But the most bizarre thing . . ."

She lowered her tone and leaned over, exposing her chest.

"That funny kid touched me, and I wonder . . . Well . . . That winter, that winter when it was so cold, if you can believe it, that's when Jack Junior finally decided to show up in my stomach . . . Yes, the next summer, I was a mother. We had tried everything, and then, out of nowhere, bingo. It's stupid, but I can't help thinking it's related . . . Maybe the child was some kind of imp?

Apparently there used to be a lot around here once upon a time, before they withdrew into the deep woods . . . So, why not? In any case, there's the proof."

And she turned to smile at a boy, about seven years old, who was teaching the alphabet to a handful of illiterate regular bar customers.

Jalibert, astonished, forgot the yellow spit and downed his beer in one gulp.

AT THE FOUNDATION

YES, THIS JALIBERT WAS A funny fellow . . . Clever enough to figure out the Humphrey connection but too stupid to make anything of it: He had come and told him everything. Just like that. Without asking for a thing. Caravelle smiled with pity.

When the detective knocked on Miss Humphrey's door, he was told that the mistress of the house had gone to spend some time in her country home on the recommendation of her doctors and wasn't accepting any visitors.

The detective was extremely frustrated by this; he had gotten all dressed up to meet this high-society big wig! He had heard so much about her when he used to spend time with the Foundation's secretary, John. He took it as a personal affront and, vexed, informed the maid that this wasn't a courtesy visit but a police investigation.

Rosalie was quite irritated. Perhaps he could leave her a message? Or speak to the secretary, Professor John, who was trusted by the family.

Professor John . . . The name was another blow to him. Caravelle remembered with nostalgia their nights of conversation over his delicious cherry brandy. From one day to the next, the scientist had stopped inviting him over. He had supposedly thrown himself body and soul into the Foundation. The memory of the insult made Caravelle's perfumed mustache quiver, but he still managed to write a dignified and perfectly professional note to explain the purpose of his visit. He asked Miss Humphrey to report to his office right away so that they could discuss the various questions he had.

The very next day, his courier brought him a letter. A rich paper covered in a neat, round handwriting. It said:

Detective,

Allow me to answer by letter the missive you deemed it appropriate to send me. I don't think a trip to the station is necessary. In fact, my doctors have ordered me to complete bed rest, and in any event I have nothing new to tell you.

The hypothesis that my brother had an illegitimate child is not only absurd, it is also ridiculous and slanderous. I beg you, with all my sister's heart, to keep it to yourself in order to spare my brother's memory and our respectable family name.

Additionally, I am in fragile health, and the disappearance of my beloved brother was a terrible blow that has considerably weakened my strength and will. Today I am only barely emerging from that horrific emptiness his absence has plunged me into by devoting myself entirely to good deeds. I ask you to respect this painful mourning with your discretion.

Thank you in advance for your understanding. Sending you, Detective, my best and most respectful wishes.

H. H.

Caravelle nearly swallowed his pipe: who did she think she was! Those rich people were unbearable, acting so untouchable. He paced around his large office three times. His cane amplified each of his gestures, his twirls turning to slashes of the air.

A challenge, yes, a real slap in the face. And he used to think those people trusted him, perhaps even thought of him as a friend. Hadn't they given him cherry brandy from the trees on their property? Didn't that mean anything?

But now Madam refused to budge, Madam had nothing to say, Madam was a wimp, Madam this and Madam that. It was out of the question for him to travel there just to be rebuffed once again. This affair had driven him up the wall enough already.

Now, he would kick things up a notch.

Unleash a storm.

Madam wanted calm? Well Madam would get what she deserved.

LEAVE

THE MOMENT HAD COME FOR him to leave. Father Bertrand knew it, and it saddened him.

He who always professed the necessity of not being taken prisoner by objects, he who always harped on about how wisdom lies in the absence of attachment, now found himself in the same trap. God, it was difficult to leave his house and his books!

He ran his hand over a row. Thick or slim, ancient or new, they all had a supple and springy leather cover, tender to the touch. There were vibrant, almost flamboyant reds, more modest burgundies, dreamy blues, imperial greens, discreet browns, austere blacks.

His finger stopped at Saint Augustine. Yes, that's what he needed to regain his courage. He took out the volume. It opened itself to pages read and reread countless times.

Earthly attachments, these invisible weights that restrain man's footsteps, could be split into four basic categories: the desire to possess, the desire to govern, the desire to love, and the desire to know. The poor mortal believed that through these means, he could take some of God's power. But it was all nothing but an illusion, vanitas vanitatum, vanity of vanities, those meager conquests that evaporated with death.

Father Bertrand looked around him. His own sin was the desire to know. Unless it was the desire to love. All those books, all his research, all that science was in fact tightly linked to his love for humanity. Myths, religions, philosophical systems constituted the cement of humankind. It was the extraordinary capacity to tell oneself stories that truly defines a human, much more than the size of his brain or his spinal column.

He started to pick out a few books that might be useful to him. He brought several story collections, ancient histories of Brittany, a work of Greek mythology, and a few books on religion, mainly primitive ones. He also added the latest scientific publications, those of his dear Darwin of course, and other lesser-known ones. He also could not bear to part with his own manuscript, a summary of demonology that he was in the process of writing. Finally, he added Saint Augustine. He looked to that funny saint, with his doubt and anger, as a sort of older brother. Leaving him behind would be too painful. Omnia vanitas, certainly, but oh well.

After some difficulty, he managed to shut his suitcase full of books.

On the other hand, he had taken no clothing.

He wouldn't need any where he was going.

ON THE ATTACK

SO CARAVELLE WENT ON THE attack. Things would not stop here. The lady wanted him to shut up? She didn't want to answer his questions? Others would do so for her. She would see what he thought of her discretion. He launched a large-scale missing person investigation.

He ordered a group of his men to return to the Daughters of Saint Agnes orphanage. They were accompanied by an excellent illustrator fresh out of the academy, who immediately set to work on a portrait of the little girl. Despite the contradicting contradictions of testimonies which were themselves contradictory, they managed to extract a few agreed-upon features, and the entire convent concurred that the final result was a fairly good likeness.

This facial composite was posted on the walls of every police station. They also sent it to the press, who circulated the image.

They decided to keep the messaging consistent so that rumors didn't spread in all directions. The line was the following: Manon, secret daughter of the lamented Professor Humphrey, was living somewhere in England without knowing the truth about her birth. The misfortunes of a little rich girl was sure to make tongues wag.

The old woman thought about slitting Caravelle's throat, but things had already gone far enough. She was forced to be on the same page and even had to publicly thank the civil servant for his devotion. He would get what was coming to him . . . Since everyone believed the professor had a daughter, they all expected her to play the role of grieving aunt. The last thing she needed was to come off as an insensitive monster, an inheritance hunter ready to deprive a defenseless orphan. She started to look for the child frantically. A tear came even came to her eye when they evoked the potential existence of this unexpected niece. What a delight in her old age!

The journalists latched onto the story with avid zeal: a little orphan the day before Christmas, they had struck gold! Each day brought a new article full of juicy details.

They all added their own flair, mixing in a touch of truth now and then.

And it was precisely this truth that might prove deadly.

When you go looking for skeletons in the closet, you might wind up a corpse yourself.

Death can be contagious.

MOLLY'S INVESTIGATION

MOLLY HIT THE SIDEWALK DETERMINED to find out whose portrait was in the little kid's file. Top hat and elegant jacket was the start of a clue, wasn't it? The first words she uttered set the gossip machine in motion. Two hours later, she knew the whole story. Well, the whole story that was going around . . . Manon, a rich heiress hunted by bad luck?

It was tempting, of course. But Molly hadn't believed in fairy tales for many long years. Before bringing Manon to the cops, washed, coiffed, and polished, she intended to find out the truth.

So the Humphrey family and the aunt, the sole inheritor known to this day, had no idea this niece existed?

A tearful aunt, so rich and so lonely, who had waited until now to circulate a portrait. Even worse! As far as Molly understood, it was the police who had set off the firecracker . . . A wet firecracker, though: after the festivities, everything would be forgotten!

Molly ruminated over these dark thoughts, walking toward Sir Humphrey's Foundation. From time to time she kicked at a stray snowflake. The snow was gray and ugly. She wanted to go back home.

Deep down, she wasn't sure she wanted to know the truth. She had grown attached to the kid, who seemed happy in her home . . . After all, if she got excited about a raw potato, who was to say she'd be happier with the bourgeois? Does a potato taste better served on porcelain and eaten with silverware?

Molly tried to imagine the girl in a living room decorated with tapestries and chandeliers and family portraits . . . No, truly, it didn't add up.

Grumbling, Molly arrived in front of the immense building.

Despite herself, she let out a whistle of admiration. Holy smokes, it was beautiful! Immense glass galleries with columns no thicker than the legs of her table. And it was tall, so tall. No doubt about it, people were doing cool things nowadays when they had the means.

Molly, with her professional gall, was preparing to address the doorman when she noticed the huge portrait hanging over the entryway.

She was so stupid! That was the man from the file! Professor Humphrey! He resembled the portrait as much as a drop of water can look like a drop of water. And the drop of water, pardon, the guy, clearly had the same forehead, the same cheeks, the same gaze as the little girl. No two ways about it, this gentleman was definitely Manon's father. It was the confirmation she had been looking for.

Her heart sank.

FRONT-PAGE NEWS

MERRY CHRISTMAS, MANON!

The young heiress of the Humphrey Foundation has just been found: she has been living for years in an underprivileged suburb of the city with a humble family of workers. Up till now she's been an orphan, a poor little girl taken care in by her generous host family, but a neighbor recognized the etching in our newspaper and called our editor. An investigative journalist hurried to the scene to verify the information, and it's with great pride and just as much emotion that the *Daily Telegraph* announces today that little Manon Humphrey will have a Christmas worthy of her rank this year. A more complete portrait of this remarkable child and the details of her extraordinary life on page 7.

VERIFICATION

"WHAT ABSOLUTE IDIOT MORONS!"

Jalibert tossed his toast aside with rage and quickly commandeered the first car he found in the street. The *Daily Telegraph* had given the exact address, what stupidity! In five minutes he was on the scene. A dense crowd of journalists and rubberneckers had beaten him there.

"What absolute idiot morons!"

Jalibert had nothing against these people in particular, but he couldn't stand the herd mentality. Masses frightened him because they were prone to troubling, irrational, and violent reactions. He took a few deep breaths before mingling into the crowd.

He was moving at the speed of a injured snail. Halfway there, he decided to take out his police badge to carve a path up to the apartment. He knocked vigorously on the thin wooden door.

A man with a sinister-looking face came to open it for him.

"Journalists have to wait their turn in line or pay a fee."

He pointed his thumb at the neighboring apartment where a more orderly line had formed, then closed the door in the detective's face. Obviously the building had found a way to make a profit off their new local curiosity: they were charging for interviews with the little girl!

Jalibert knocked on the door three more times even more violently, and when the nasty guy's head appeared in the doorway again, he shoved his police badge under his nose, and his revolver, too, for good measure. The guy took a step back with his arms up. Clearly, this wasn't his first police raid. He assumed a cooperative expression and led Jalibert to the main room.

It was a humble living room with a wood-burning stove. They had obviously tried to improve the interior a bit: a doily had been strewn over a dilapidated couch and artificial flowers were sitting in a vase on the table. Jalibert would have been willing to bet that two days earlier, the room had been covered in bottles of beer and dirty ashtrays.

A little girl was seated near the stove. Her eyes were red, her hair white—and it was not Manon.

The newspapers didn't have all the information. Most importantly, they didn't know the little girl was mute. The fake Manon was recounting her life in great detail to the journalist. She had clearly memorized her speech, and a large woman with a ruddy nose was watching her to make sure she made no blunders.

These monsters had nabbed a little albino girl somewhere and trained her so that they could claim the large inheritance promised to the daughter of Professor Humphrey.

Jalibert took out his handcuffs and arrested the two crooks. He had no desire to beat around the bush. They had ruined his morning, after all.

He was gentler with the child, but he still had to bring her to the station: in taking on Manon's identity, she was also taking on Manon's enemies. She needed to be watched for a few days, just enough time for the misunderstanding to be cleared up.

When he arrived at the station, he saw that a few other little girls with red eyes had also been brought in, and even a few little boys. Everyone was trying their luck, just in case, why not? All of the men under Detective Caravelle were put in charge of protecting these little counterfeits, and the investigation took a serious blow.

"What absolute idiot morons!" was the only comment Jalibert offered the journalists swarming at the station doors.

The next day, the *Daily Telegraph* retracted its statement and offered a flimsy excuse to its readers. But the affair had been juicy: the revenue they made on those two papers guaranteed its editors a comfortable Christmas vacation.

A COAT

AT THE HEART OF THE Foundation, in the splendid solarium on the floor reserved for management, the tension was palpable.

How did this happen? How, how, how? John was pacing around the large oak desk.

How, how, how?

The name Humphrey was plastered on every newspaper! Every employee, every employee's wife, every cousin of an employee's wife was now aware of the existence of the little girl!

John was still pacing, and Miss Humphrey, seated on the desk, was beginning to feel slightly nauseous. She took a long puff from her cigarette holder, leaving a trace of greasy lipstick. She gently blew out the smoke, but that didn't appease her.

The secretary, paying her no mind, continued to walk the hundred steps of the office spouting his litany.

Thank God people were too stupid to put two and two together . . . But if, by chance, someone figured out what was really going on . . . One of those nosy journalists for example. It would be catastrophic! Catastrophic!

The woman spat up another puff of smoke and decided it was time to intervene.

"Catastrophic, you say, dear! Do you know what my tailor said to me this morning?"

Clearly John wasn't listening, lost in his own thoughts. Miss Humphrey grabbed him by the tie and pulled him to face her. John was too surprised to react. Their faces were nearly glued together; he smelled the odor of tobacco mixed with the thick and complicated perfume she used in abundance. She repeated her question in a hiss.

Did he know what her tailor had said to her that morning? No, of course he didn't know. How could he know?

The tailor had refused to prepare the incredible mink coat she had planned to wear for the Christmas gala at the Sisters of the Cross. Miss Humphrey was choking on her rage, and John caught a whiff of her heavy breath, charged with hatred. He managed to free himself from her grasp.

Miss Humphrey, fuming, continued her lament:

"And do you know why he refused?"

John, busy redoing the knot of his tie, didn't respond and left her question hanging. He had a vague idea of the answer this time. The reason was Manon. He tried to distract her:

"Don't tell me those moron animal protectors have decided it's immoral to gas minks to take their skin?"

The previous winter, a group of zealots had passionately protested against the barbaric use of feathers and pelts for fashion, claiming it was an absurd and cruel luxury at the expense of the poor creatures. Harriet had laughed at first, but the Plumage League had grown in size, and she'd had to give up her splendid boas for fear of scandal. Since then, she hadn't stopped talking about it. But she was worried about something far more serious this time, and the distraction didn't work.

"The tailor refused to extend me credit under the pretext that my inheritance is no longer guaranteed! Can you imagine? The newspapers pull a kid from behind a dumpster, and now I don't get to have a mink vest like Miss Rose's!"

The older woman paused, took one more drag from her cigarette-holder and then crushed the butt with a face full of contempt.

"We have no choice, John. We have to get rid of her as soon as possible. Give the order. Kill her in some accident, and make sure her body is found so that this case can finally be closed."

John stood back up. He scrutinized her. Was she serious?

She was.

The public believed little Manon was a potential illegitimate daughter . . . They wanted her to have the inheritance . . . They were calling her house, her lifestyle, her wardrobe into question!

She ran her hand through her bun. The aggravation was making her itch.

John was speechless. The millions attached to the Humphrey name were nothing in comparison to the treasures the little girl was hiding. Revolutionary discoveries! As long as she was alive, she represented enormous potential! Enormous!

These discoveries needed to be preserved.

Miss Humphrey was categorical: she would preserve whatever he liked, but only in the same mink coat as Miss Rose.

Dear Charles,

Each species, each race, has its own survival system adapted to its environment. Some choose to go on the attack as predators. They no longer fear other animals, but have a need for large amounts of energy and find themselves at the mercy of hunger. Other species prefer to save their energy and opt for defensive behavior. They are a priori more fragile, but nature gives them other weapons. Camouflage, for example. Thus numerous animals have a color that allows them to blend into their landscape.

The landscape, however, can change. Take the birch moth, from the Greek phalaina, *the "night butterfly."*

This butterfly rests on trees during the day. There are two kinds: one that's nearly black, and another that's lighter. The light moths used to exist in much greater numbers, because they were less noticeable on the white wood of birch trees and were thus attacked less often by predators. But then something happened: pollution darkened the trees around the big cities, and now the white butterflies, which have become very visible, are easy pray for the birds. The black moths are better equipped to survive.

And man? Man has lost his fur. As an individual, he has become vulnerable in nature. But man has built himself a far more powerful organization: society. It's society that serves as his environment today, society that creates its own rules of attack and defense. Fashion plays a primordial role in this: the color of a coat now allows us to act discreetly or, on the contrary, to put ourselves on display to be noticed by our peers.

Selection has become cultural. It is no less merciless.

Your friend H.

MEETING

When she returned home, Molly had a hard time getting her words out. She rambled chaotically, often privileging rhyme over meaning. Manon managed to understand two things: Molly was emotional, and she had to go to the Humphrey Foundation.

So the little girl went to the Foundation.

But not alone! Giulio insisted on accompanying her, and Molly insisted on accompanying Giulio.

It was the first time Manon had stepped foot back outside. She had grown used to the confined space of Molly's room, and the abrupt change of scale made her dizzy. Like when you're swimming in the ocean and you suddenly become aware of how much water is around you. She was trembling slightly. She clung even more tightly to Molly's skirts.

"Are you cold, little one? Take my shawl, it's not exactly new, but the best soups are made in old shawls, as they say."

No, Manon was not cold, but the feel of the yellow shawl, flimsy but warm and soft, was like a balm over her heart. She clung to it as to a life preserver and finally dared to look around her.

The city had barely changed since her escape from the orphanage. The snow had left white stains on the windows and roofs, but there was still a dreadful gray cast over everything. The melted snow had mixed with the blackish sludge of the main avenues and was flowing into the gutter with a sickly slowness. Here, nature always seemed in agony.

In the street, families took advantage of the respite to make their Christmas preparations. This was obviously the more well off part of the city, inhabited by people who had money to spend on things other than food and protection from the cold. The children, dressed in nice wool coats, pulled their mothers by the hand, leading the group toward this or that store with tantalizing window displays. Just behind followed the fathers who were usually inspecting their shoes or cleaning their pipes. Finally, the servants closed up the rear, carrying stacks of vibrant boxes or clusters of multicolored bags.

A band of dirty children in rags came out of nowhere. Like little devils, they charged across the street at full speed, carrying off a few packages with them. The bourgeois cursed them. Two police officers went running after them, already flushed with the effort. Giulio, thinking it was a game, started to chase the officers. Molly laughed. She was against the police on principle, although many of her clients were policeman she was fond of . . .

Manon was fascinated by all the commotion. She was starting to enjoy the spectacle when she noticed a funny individual on the other side of the street, half hidden in a dark alley. A very tall man, very thin, very pale. He wore giant round black glasses and yet, she could feel his two eyes riveted on her. He was watching her, she was sure of it.

A passing car nearly splashed Manon. She was only distracted for a fraction of a second, but the strange beanpole had disappeared.

She nearly jumped when she saw him a second later standing opposite her. How had he crossed the street so quickly? Now there could be no doubt: the man was watching her and smiling at her. Manon moved even closer to Molly's enormous petticoat, wishing she could melt into it.

The man approached her. He was now very close, very, very close. He lifted his left hand in a large, elegant gesture and brought it to the little girl's face. Just above her, she saw his long and slender fingers with their polished white nails. A discolored spider. Like in a nightmare, everything seemed to be happening in slow motion. Molly noticed nothing, how was that possible? Manon wanted to cry out, but she could only squeeze herself tighter against her protector and shut her eyes. That's when she heard very distinctly, deep in her heart, two words that echoed on and on:

"Little sister . . . Little sister . . . Little sister . . . Little sister . . . Little sister . . ."

It was Molly who woke her from her torpor, shaking her by the shoulder. The words, this time, were very real, chiming, off-kilter:

"Pfft! Hey, kid! Look, isn't that something!"

Manon opened her eyes again. The voice inside her quieted. The man had disappeared.

Dear Charles,

I'm trying to explain to my hosts the defining features of our civilization, and it's a completely fascinating exercise . . . Where to begin? The arts? The law? The idea of God, perhaps? I finally opted for a more modest entry point: the grain of wheat.

Yes, wheat, one of the three important cereals that has nourished mankind for centuries: wheat in Europe, rice in Asia, corn in America. Wheat constitutes seventy-five percent of the daily nutrition for everyday families. I explained to them that it is consumed most often in the form of bread. How we finely crush the grains to obtain flour, then add water and a bit of yeast. How the little ferments contained in it allow the dough to rise in order to form the soft crumbs. How we leave the dough to rest for several hours before putting it in the oven.

Yeast is simply made from a mix of flour and water that we leave to ferment in a sufficiently warm place. The presence of food, water, and heat allows for the creation of little bacteria: the lactobacillus. We made some together, and their yeast starter is ready. All you have to do is feed the flour regularly and take a bit of yeast to make the bread when needed. Having a few grains of wheat handy thus means possessing in seedling form the foundations of our alimentary culture.

Your friend H.

FINALLY!

FINALLY, LBN HAD MANAGED TO make contact! Ecstatic, he did a little dance, and then promptly collapsed.

Fortunately, there hadn't been any passersby in that dark alley. He could rest on the ground for a few minutes . . .

His vision was blurry, his movements feverish. He was listening to the beating of his heart, which had slowed considerably. Winter was here, he couldn't ignore it any longer. Lbn carefully stood up and wrapped his immense scarf back around him.

These last few weeks had been particularly grueling.

He had approached Molly's window several times but had never achieved contact. The little girl wasn't at all receptive.

Maybe that stemmed from her nature, or else her mind was too occupied. Or maybe it was that he was already too weak.

He had to preserve his energy if he wanted to fulfill his mission.

And then there was Giulio . . . The dog, who had started out as his precious helper, now seemed more and more reticent. Lbn knew exactly what was happening: the animal was jealous.

One cannot live in human society without suffering the consequences. Sooner or later, humankind's vices rub off onto those around them. The dog, the animal closest to them, had been affected by greed. Then, over time, he had learned the concept of possession. No doubt the worst human flaw, the one that makes them believe they are the owners of the earth, the one responsible for the majority of wars.

Giulio had decided that the little girl belonged to him, and Lbn had become his rival.

He looked around for which way to go. A few meters away, a little door led to a cellar. With some difficulty, he managed to stand up. His long legs struggled to support his weight. His knees had a mind of their own. Staggering along, he reached the old wooden door. Luckily, the lock was flimsy. He picked it with the tip of his index finger, opened the door a crack, and slipped inside.

He happily inhaled the slightly earthy odor. The air was warmer, more humid. His eyes rested in the darkness of the room. He felt better already. His vigor was returning, but he couldn't overestimate his strength.

In a particularly dark corner, he noticed a family of rats. He approached gently, extending the ashen palm of his left hand.

The largest of the rats sniffed it for a minute before climbing on. With his right hand, Lbn rifled in his pocket. He took out a few grains of wheat. He always had some on him now, just in case. He offered them to the little rodent, whose nose wriggled for another few minutes. Finally, Lbn dozed off in a ball at their side. His body formed a perfect circle.

He fell asleep satisfied: contact had been established; she could no longer escape him.

BOOK SIX

Dear Charles,

You know how proud I was of my little civilization course . . . I certainly didn't expect the reaction I got! The Council of Elders came in person to destroy our starter yeast in a dark rage, and have confiscated my grains of wheat.

My beautiful angel explained to me that they deem agriculture against nature: domesticating the earth is about domination, and their society has no tolerance for that. Their lifestyle depends on a fragile equilibrium with no reserves. Like tightrope walkers, they are always on the edge of the precipice. An overly dry or overly wet spring means their year must be devoted entirely to the search for food. They only have a few months to amass the necessary energy, for winter weakens their strength. Their bodies conserve energy, like animals that spend the harshest months of the year in hibernation.

Thus their life revolves around their natural needs, and any attempt to stockpile or save is absolutely prohibited. That might seem ridiculous to us, but it's a tried and true system: this civilization, if I've understood correctly, is several million years old, and thriving! While ours, though much younger, is already in bad shape . . . Factories multiply in the suburbs of the city, poor people live in the poisonous smoke, while the rich drown in sugar and surplus. The race for profit has rendered us insane, and today each person feels entitled to trample his neighbor in order to gain a few extra pounds sterling. Yes, our alimentary equilibrium now depends on ecological, political, and ethical aberrations that we'll have to pay for sooner or later.

Also, I fear I have sown discord by telling them about wheat . . . Everyone has docilely followed the orders of the Elders, but a certain tension remains and I suspect a few young ones have sneakily saved a few grains. I have to be very careful so as not to destroy their delicate system.

Your friend H.

THE FOUNDATION

MANON, GIULIO, AND MOLLY SOON find themselves in front of the large glass building that had so amazed the plump poetess.

Manon was also impressed . . . impressed and charmed. It was immense, luminous, marvelous. Here the light was in its palace. The metallic structures looked like the veins of an immense leaf turned toward the brightness of the day. Yes, she felt it: the man who had conceived of this building could have been her father.

For the first time in her life, her heart simmered with pride.

Giulio had reappeared. Molly gave him a signal to stay outside, and she led the little girl by the hand.

The door imitated the style of ancient temples: two columns of fine copper bore a vast pediment built in an immense and pure mirror. Underneath were big golden letters displaying the name and motto of the grounds:

HUMPHREY FOUNDATION

Science and Conscience

Together, they walked through the huge panels of the entryway.

A vestibule helped to maintain the indoor temperature. Large copper tubes allowed for ventilation. A thick braided bamboo rug kept the floor insulated. On the glass walls, large raw-silk curtains diffused the light. Thus neither the temperature nor the luminosity could aggress the living beings that inhabited the building: the plants, the animals, the humans. Everything seemed designed to live in harmony with its milieu.

But upon entering the building, Manon was quickly disillusioned: its appearance was extraordinary, but its purpose, on the other hand, was monstrous. As far as the eye could see: cadavers.

1347

1347 was hungry.

He felt the burn in the hollow of his stomach; soon he wouldn't be able to resist anymore.

The granule dispenser was in the corner. All he had to do was approach and press one of those large buttons, green or red. It seemed so simple . . . But it wasn't. Because every other time when he hit one of those buttons, it unleashed an electrical current that coursed through his back. He would feel his spine break and be paralyzed from the pain. Each time, 1347 thought that his hour had come, that this shock would be the last. He would have hoped for it if his survival instinct hadn't been inscribed in him so deeply. But in the end, he got up. And now the hunger had returned.

At the beginning, it was simple: the green button meant food, the red button meant the electric shock. It had lasted a good week, then, when he was starting to gain confidence, the logic had been scrambled.

The red, the green, the green, the red, the red, the red . . . The electricity and the granules had become interchangeable, random, senseless, hopeless.

The men in white shirts were testing his intelligence. 1347 had never been taken for a particularly brilliant rat, nor was he completely stupid, but what he really didn't understand was the cruelty of those humans.

He had watched his mother die of exhaustion, the sweet 1332, and he knew that soon it would be his turn. And he didn't understand why.

But he was hungry.

1347 timidly approached the dispenser. He grazed the two buttons with his whiskers. No, nothing distinguished them, apart from the color. Both were connected to the large transparent container full of granules. He hesitated for a long while, trying to find a way to get into the container. A waste of time, he knew he didn't have the choice. He had to choose red . . . or green . . . or red.

Red. His favorite color, the color of 1332's eyes.

The electric shock made him gasp, and he rested, breathless, on the wood chips in the large cage. His heart raced frantically in his little chest, completely out of control. Suddenly, it stopped. This time, 1347 would not get back up.

The laboratory assistant gathered the cadaver and took note of the animal's numerous hesitations. He was satisfied: clearly, the rat had understood that there was danger involved.

In his place he set down another tiny little rat, 1356.

BY THE THOUSANDS

MANON SHIVERED.

The cadavers were lined up along the thin glass walls.

Bodies of all sizes and all colors were pinned in neat rows. Wooden boxes tried to dress up this horrific carnage as a semblance of art.

Here were sumptuous butterflies with wings of an unreal blue, still gleaming, as though ready to fly away. Others, slightly more violet, were outlined with an elegant deep black. Next to them, another set of smaller butterflies flashed hints of fiery red, orange, gold.

On the walls of the Foundation was all of nature's palette: magenta, carmine, saffron, Aegean or Prussian blue, pearl gray, lavender, dusty pink, chocolate, burnt Sienna . . . And black, which in light strokes gave the ensemble its structure and dynamism.

On the opposite wall were the moths, the night butterflies. Although less conspicuous than their daytime cousins, they are in fact more numerous and more ancient. Some of their ancestors had even fluttered around dinosaurs.

"Notice the difference between the antennae: the Rhopalocera, the butterflies, have real antennae while the moths, the Heterocera, have feather-type things on their heads. They're better at capturing pheromones, these chemical messages their fellow moths send them."

Molly had started to follow an instructor who was teaching a class of young boys the basics of entomology, the science of insects. Most of them were busy picking their noses or scratching the scabs on their knees. Very few were listening to the professor, only Molly was paying attention, and the professor ended up turning his attention to the large eccentric lady so that his lessons didn't fall completely on deaf ears.

"Tell me, boys, is the spider an insect?"

A student knocked off the hat of his shorter neighbor, who elbowed him in the stomach. Molly ventured a timid nod of her head . . .

"Well actually, it's not! Look closely. Here, on the left, a specimen from the arachnid family . . . A spider. And here, look at that row of insects of all kinds. How is the spider different?"

The taller kid stomped on the shorter one's foot, who had to bite his hand not to scream. Molly shrugged her shoulders in a sign of ignorance; she didn't see the difference.

"Count their legs!"

The short one's friend grabbed the taller one's underpants, which were sticking out, and yanked them as hard as he could. The taller one squirmed, the two short ones laughed. Molly counted the legs.

"Take note: spiders have eight legs, insects have six."

Another tall kid strangled the little avenger, and the friend, as retaliation, smeared a booger on the jacket of the original tormenter.

Molly nodded her head and turned toward Manon. "You hear that, kid? Eight legs for spiders, sorry, for arachnids, and six legs for insects! Good to know, huh?"

Manon wasn't really interested, but she gave a small forced smile. She didn't want to tarnish her companion's good mood . . . But she would have given anything to leave.

A student from the group was less diplomatic. He said, a little too loudly:

"Who cares about insects, this is torture."

The old professor nearly throttled him. "You don't care? You don't care? Do you know that insects make up seventy-five percent of the living world? Yes, seventy-five percent! While vertebrates, that branch we're all so crazy about, represents only six percent! And that's including the whale, the stork, the mouse, the snake, the carp, and, of course, your cousin the monkey!"

The class burst into laughter. And when he had finished his rant and turned his back to continue his lecture, the professor was followed by twenty students imitating chimpanzees.

Molly watched them walk away with a look of dismay.

Manon, despite herself, was riveted by the multicolored carcasses. She couldn't tear her gaze away from the thousands of tiny agonies proudly exhibited for the eyes of hobbyists and school kids.

Below each little cadaver, a faded slip of paper gave the scientific name of the specimen as well as its current denomination.

These withered labels reminded her of her own file, the one she had left at the apartment out of caution, and her shiver of disgust morphed into a trembling.

Her back started to hurt again. A muted pain twisted through her shoulder blades. She felt as though she too were pinned, attached to these walls which an hour earlier had been unknown to her.

This place smelled like hatred. Reeked of it.

What had she come looking for here? What was she hoping for exactly?

Manon concentrated on her shoes, trying not to faint.

Staring at the floor, she noticed something that no other visitor had noticed: on the ground, by the hundreds, by the thousands, by the hundred thousands, ants were swarming.

1356

1356 found life pretty easy.

As soon as he was hungry, he pressed on the large green button and the machine immediately served him a copious amount of granules. He had made the mistake of pressing on the red button once, but he had learned his lesson and wouldn't do that again!

1356 had just finished his meal and was about to take a nice nap. It was his stomach's turn to work now, his brain and muscles now had to recuperate. He dug a small comfortable hole in the wood chips and rolled up in it with pleasure.

Yes, life was pretty easy. Not exciting, but not horrible either.

Sleep was settling its calming wings over the little rat when a noise abruptly struck his ear, reverberating inside of his minuscule body:

"Leave! Leave! Leave!"

The rodent flipped over himself and flattened his front paws over his ears, as though trying to fold them down. The voice, however, persisted:

"Leave! Leave! Leave!"

He half stood, his gaze dark and his brow furrowed. These humans and their stupid tests were so annoying! He would leave, fine, after his nap.

But his eyes were starting to get used to the images in his cage, and he noticed that it wasn't one of the men in white shirts who was speaking to him, but a little monkey with a funny-looking face. It took 1356 a few minutes to realize that they had cut and restitched a part of its skull. The stitches were crude and its head was terribly swollen in places.

1356 eked out a feeble:

"But . . . l-l-leave to do what?"

"Leave!" the young chimpanzee repeated.

"Leave!" confirmed a rabbit that had appeared out of nowhere. Its eyes, red and oozing, had doubled in size as a result of some kind of infection.

"Leave!" insisted a mouse with wings carved into it, whose scars were still fresh.

Leave! Leave!

And all together they pushed the cage.

Leave! Leave!

The cage tipped over, and 1356 was out.

Leave! Leave!

1356 helped the group push over the neighboring cage.

Perched on top of a cabinet, behind his black glasses, Lbn was leading the operation.

AGITATION

JOHN, AGITATED, CONTINUED TO PACE around his office. Obviously things were not going according to plan . . .

He was one of those men of action who think that good ideas only come while walking. He was suspicious of ideas that came when he was sitting, or worse, lying down. The brain needs oxygen, and immobility, which he conflated with death, could only lend itself to putrid thoughts.

But he sometimes paused his frantic movements so he could scratch himself. Stress did strange things to him. He was never objectively worried. Not in a conscious way. But as soon as he found himself in a difficult situation, he became covered in red patches that itched terribly. It was unpleasant, but it had stopped concerning him a long time ago.

He paused once more to scratch behind his knee.

Miss Humphrey had lit another cigarette. But smoking was less pleasant around that unbearable itching. She wasn't used to it. In stressful situations, she settled for being obnoxious, which allowed her to take it out on someone else while she waited for her calm to be restored.

But scratching, no, that was not at all dignified!

She had always scolded John for it, it was ridiculous! And now he was contorting in all directions like an old baboon!

"John, stop doing tha—"

In a fraction of a second, she had turned as white as her cigarette. Her lower lip was trembling from a nervous tic.

"J . . . J . . ."

"Yes, dear? What, what is it?"

"J . . . J . . . John, you're covered in fleas! It's revolting! Abhorrent! Sickening! Vile!"

The lady was nearly having a stroke, and he didn't dare tell her that he could see fleas tumbling from her own hair . . . He simply shimmied even more to escape the bites of all those tiny vampires.

The fleas were jumping everywhere, and Miss Humphrey took a few steps back to avoid them. She heard a very clear crunch that started from her left heel and climbed along her leg, then her pelvis, then her spine. She had just crushed something. She looked down.

A long line of spiders was crossing the office, and a few had started to climb up her ankle. Miss Humphrey let out a scream that was so loud John thought he'd gone deaf. He caught her before she fainted, and together they ran for the exit.

But they were stopped by a large languid body.

Dear Charles,

The Council of Elders decided to interrogate me about our civilization. I felt like I was in a courtroom, and I confess that a number of their questions embarrassed me, especially those about how we care for our weakest, and sometimes I toned down the truth so as not to make us seem like horrible brutes. Slavery is a horror, the place of women is a scandal, our tyranny over childhood is shameful, not to mention how we treat beings of other species! Breeding, slaughtering, experimental treatments, sordid games involving animal suffering . . .

As a man of heart and reason, you were one of the first to critique vivisection. It took me some time to understand you, to support you, to follow you. Why? What mechanism renders us so insensitive to the suffering of others? No one inflicts pain for the pleasure of it, and it's in the name of progress that we have started to use animals in laboratories . . . Progress for what, for whom, and at what price? 90% of tests that have worked on animals have turned out to be ineffective on humans. But logic was pushed aside, habit took over, laws engraved barbarity in marble. Why measure the toxicity of domestic products in the eyes of rabbits? And why do we perform psychological experiments to determine the intelligence of such and such a species? Do we think that by torturing them we can better understand them? What do we learn from the dogs that we make jump onto electric hot plates so we can record the precise moment when they stop hoping and let themselves die? Horror has become systemic: from the simple student completing his first dissections to the greatest scholar publishing articles full of data, today all research leaves a bloodbath in its wake.

To understand the process of aging, pigs are regularly burned: we tear off pieces of skin, wait for it to scar, and begin again. It's one way of studying our tissue's capacity for renewal, and also of finding the right substance to add to firming cream to make it more effective. This is the price we pay for the illusion of looking a bit younger in the mirror . . . But who still dares to look at their reflection?

Your friend H.

WIND OF MADNESS

JOHN WAS ON THE GROUND staring at a foot that did not belong to Miss Humphrey. The socks were stretched over a calf that was much too hairy.

It was the calf of the laboratory assistant.

John stood up and sharply reprimanded him. What if he had been carrying something dangerous? Science required caution . . .

He even seemed to have forgotten the fleas.

The poor boy listened docilely, but he was pacing nervously without even realizing it, clearly worked up over something. Finally John asked him what he wanted. The young man took a deep breath and began.

The research lab had been turned upside down. The animals had suddenly become uncontrollable: the rats had escaped, the butterflies had gone mad, the birds were screaming in their cages. It was a ridiculous spectacle; the asisstant had no clue what was going on. He had to come check it out.

So Miss Humphrey and John followed the young man to the laboratory to take stock of the disaster. They were not disappointed. The animals were ransacking the place.

Miss Humphrey had a new reason to tear her hair out, but John stopped scratching himself and turned to his companion with a large smile:

"The little girl has arrived."

He did a dance and headed toward his office, singing:

"The little girl has arrived, hey hey, the lit-tle gi-irl has arrived, hey hey . . ."

Miss Humphrey and the young lab assistant looked at each other, panicked. Clearly the wave of madness was spreading to humans, too.

But John was more lucid than ever. He opened the closet, rifled around for a moment, and pulled out a box of matches and a few candles that he placed around the room.

"Man's great advantage over animals is fire. Let's go, comrades."

The first wicks had barely been illuminated when the beasts started to recoil.

"Now, lock all the doors!"

He took Miss Humphrey's hand, brought it to his lips, and murmured:

"Miss, I invite you on a little hunt. Believe me, the animal we're going to trap is worth its weight in gold . . . You can use its skin to make your little coat for Miss Rose's house."

The two of them headed for the main hall.

EARLY CLOSING

MANON REALIZED THAT THE DOORS were closing when she saw the lines of ants suddenly doubling back. As incredible as it seemed, the insects seemed to be rebelling against the guards!

Manon's instinct told her to run, run as fast as possible. In her head resounded thousands of voices saying, "Leave! Leave! Leave! Leave! Leave! Leave! Leave! Leave! Leave! Leave! Leave! Leave! Leave!"

But her desire to know kept her from running away . . . She was so close to the truth! To leave now would mean starting again from zero . . . Manon, among mankind for too long, had caught their stupid vanity. Who cares about knowledge when it's a matter of life and death?

"Vanitas vanitatum, et omnia vanitas," the large boy with black glasses remarked to himself before silently screaming a resounding "LEAVE" at Manon.

Molly, imperturbable, was admiring the glass display cases. She studied the various kinds of insects, marveled over their tiny variations. She took in all the colors, textures, and shapes, excited to use them in her future poetic endeavors. Molly hadn't seen all the ants on the ground and was paying no attention to the impromptu closing of the doors. It was a sharp pain in her hand that wrested her from her contemplation.

Manon was so on edge that she was unconsciously digging her little translucent nails into her friend's reddish skin. The large woman immediately dropped her smile and tried to gauge the degree of danger.

Thousands of insects. Closed doors. Paralyzed child.

And all the exits seemed blocked.

Through the main entrance, she saw Giulio scratching desperately at the closed doors. Yes, they were in danger.

Where to go? Molly squeezed the child against her body in a gesture of illusory protection. But the ants did the same. Another minute and Manon would be covered with insects from head to toe. Molly frantically tried to chase them off.

And then a man arrived, brandishing a candlestick.

The insects backed away, and Manon let out one of those mysterious mute screams. A terrible mute scream that seemed to pierce your eardrums and brain even though no sound actually came out.

The man with the torch grabbed the little girl by the fist and forced her to follow him. Molly pushed the little girl in the man's direction. This human presence reassured her, and the man seemed to have a plan.

Indeed he did.

First things first, get rid of Molly.

GIULIO

WITH HIS CLAWS, GIULIO HAD tried to puncture the kind of transparent wall that kept him outside. Within him, he heard thousands of little voices screaming. He sensed the little girl was in danger, and he sensed his mistress couldn't help her. He tried to attack the door, but his fangs, though sturdy, slid down the glass. There was nothing he could do. Absolutely nothing.

The inaction of the passersby, especially, revolted him. He was barking as loud as he could, but those moronic humans didn't understand dog language. Instead they listened to the lie told by their fellow human:

"Stand back!" shouted the doorman. "There's been an incident, but the situation is now under control . . . Stand back! Let security do their work!"

There was whispering that one of the lions had escaped.

Giulio tried once more to force his way in and was met with a big kick to the stomach. The pain took his breath away. A strident whistling crushed his eardrums. An ultrasonic whistle. The men from the pound were on their way!

They would make him their scapegoat! Tomorrow, he would be "the incident," the newspapers would talk about a rabid dog and the case would be closed.

But Giulio knew these streets well, and it wasn't his first time leading the jailers from the pound on a wild goose chase!

His secret was tracing a path that the men couldn't follow. Women's skirts, especially, were incredibly useful. Giulio took off, passed between a pair of bourgeois legs, then a second, and before arriving at the third, his pursuers were already far behind, red with confusion and weaving between the frilly obstacles.

He turned left and right with the least logic possible, then hid himself in the first hole that presented itself. This time, Giulio waited under a stairwell for the customary half hour until the danger had passed. Then he stuck his nose out and left again down the street as if nothing had happened.

He made his way back up the main boulevard. He didn't want to do what came next, but he had no choice. The lives of Molly and the little girl were at stake. He knew it, he sensed it. The Foundation had closed like an immense mouth over his two friends, it would swallow them whole. He had to stop that from happening.

Yes, but the problem had become human, so he needed a human to resolve it. And the tall guy with the black glasses was the most humanlike acquaintance he had.

PAPERWORK

THE STATION WAS CRUMBLING UNDER so many false alarms. Caravelle loudly cursed the greediness of these people, and Jalibert quietly cursed the incompetence of his boss. With each new call, he had to open a file, go verify the information himself, post a guard just in case, close the file. It was an insane waste of time and money.

It wasn't until night that Jalibert could really study what he called "the Manon case."

Despite the energy he spent, the information remained meager. He had hardly anything that could be deemed serious besides the testimony of the nuns. And even that was dubious. The only verifiable, absolutely concrete, and indubitably real clue was the murder of the Mother Superior.

For the umpteenth time, he consulted the medical examiner's report. The old nun had been meticulously tortured. It wasn't the work of a sadist, it was the work of an expert, of someone who needed to extract information. A lot of the skin had been removed; he must have had a lot of questions. The old woman hadn't spoken right away. Either she really wanted to guard her secret, or she didn't have the answers they were looking for.

Jalibert opted for the second option. He knew that the Institute of the Daughters of Saint Agnes had nothing to do with the little girl.

He looked again at the photo of the cadaver. The quality was mediocre, but it was still clear that the incisions were impeccable and neat. The victim had been bound with thin braided ropes. An extremely sharp weapon had been used. The blade of a professional. Perhaps a butcher's tool, or a scalpel . . .

A scalpel . . . There were loads of scientific tools at the Humphrey Foundation.

Jalibert glanced at the city through the tiny skylight near his table. It was night already. Everything was calm, but he knew that the glacial December wind was whitewashing the town. He shivered with compassion for his two men who were staking out the Humphrey Foundation.

He had bypassed the approval of Caravelle, who was too busy with all the inheritance frauds, and had set up an around-the-clock guard duty.

The Foundation held the key to the mystery. It was the only thing he was really sure of at this point.

Jalibert opened the old skylight with a creak. The cold air whipped his face and he felt the wetness on his mustache freeze. It was even worse than he thought. Let's hope his men had brought hot coffee with them.

He was serving himself a large cup when someone knocked on his door.

PRESENTATIONS

MANON HADN'T REALIZED THAT HER friend had disappeared. Entirely absorbed in her own anxiety, she had let herself be dragged up to the upper floor without resisting.

The man had placed her on a cozy armchair and served her a cup of tea. For a short while, she had almost felt good.

Except for the candle still burning nearby, and the mean smile she couldn't help noticing behind his mask of friendliness. The gleam of the flame made grotesque, disturbing shadows dance across her face.

Manon forced herself to look away. She gazed down at her hands, which were trembling. But not out of fear, no. It was still, always, that pain in her shoulders that refused to leave her in peace. It was less sharp now, but also more spread out. Manon's arms went numb, and her back felt like it was confined in a corset full of sharp needles.

"Sweetheart, is she the one who brought the fleas?"

She lifted her eyes. A towering woman had just entered the office. She scrutinized the little girl with a tight-lipped expression. Manon shrank a little farther into the back of her seat. The woman's demeanor frightened her, and her perfume bothered her. She jumped when the man started to laugh, a loud, booming laugh.

"In a way, yes, you're right, my dear . . ."

"Oh, John! Spare me that big gorilla laugh and tell me what this fleabag is doing in our office."

"Haven't you guessed who our guest is? Don't you recognize her? Look at those high cheekbones, those furrowed brows . . . No, nothing?"

The woman looked at her with dismay. She wasn't used to being around tramps and she found John's insinuations quite vexing. And that little superior smile of his was unbearable.

Who did he think he was?

He was nothing but a social climber, a commoner who had only climbed the rungs of society thanks to her! She still remembered when he was just her brother's assistant . . . All the groveling he used to do to the great professor Humphrey! He was quite the boot-licker.

And then he had seduced her, and then there was "the agreement," which had intertwined their fates forever.

Who'd had the idea first? She liked to think it was her, because she imagined herself in control of her past and her future, but she wasn't sure anymore. She wanted the millions, he wanted the Foundation, so they had joined forces.

And where had that gotten her? Nowhere, to tell the truth . . . She was still the same, still in the same place. All that had changed was that she'd gained a few pounds and her conscience also weighed on her sometimes, when she was alone at night. She lit a cigarette to chase away these somber thoughts.

The lighter visibly appalled the little girl, which Miss Humphrey found amusing.

"Darling, I beg you, stop with the riddles and tell me who your new friend is."

She seemed sincere. The fat millionaire's naiveté always surprised him.

"Take a good look! It's Manon, your niece!"

Miss Humphrey's smoke went down the wrong pipe, and she suffered a monumental coughing fit.

The little girl stared at that dragon-woman and the smoke coming out of her, wide-eyed.

BOOK SEVEN

A HOPELESS SITUATION

LATER, MUCH LATER, WHEN MOLLY woke up, she was in an unknown place, she was cold and in pain.

Her head was pounding. No doubt about it, she had been hit.

She sensed an enormous bump above her neck, behind the ear. She tried to touch it, but she realized she was tied up. Thin braided ropes bound her feet and fists.

Molly recited a few lines of poetry to calm herself and analyzed the situation.

Nothing is hopeless but hopelessness.

When you break things down, it's much less of a mess.

Turns out she was a rational woman who didn't know it. This adventure had taught her plenty of new things.

Time to learn a new lesson: how to get out of a hopeless situation.

She tried to look around, but the darkness was nearly complete. She must have been in a cellar, underground, or else it was a moonless night. She tried listening to her surroundings, she needed to find a clue. Any clue. She wasn't about to let herself die like this!

She concentrated hard enough to finally grasp a noise . . . a murmur . . . a presence. Maybe it was just her imagination whispering what she wanted, but she would take it. Believing didn't necessarily solve things, but it made the wait a little less painful. Which isn't so bad in the end.

There was a presence. Voices, she was sure of it. A man and a woman. Not very far.

The man with the nice suit! How could she have trusted him? Her mother always used to say: *Man in a suit, give him the boot!* That said, her mother had a tendency to consider the entire world a pain in the butt. Men especially, and little kids . . . The little girl . . . The little girl? The little girl! Where was the little girl?

This recollection suddenly electrified her and she wriggled her wrists in their binds.

Poor kid! What had he done with her, that monstrous monster? She would make him eat his nice suit!

Where was the little girl?

The binds were tight and Molly knew her attempts were in vain. Hope is practical, but it can't be summoned just like that.

For the first time in a long time, she started to cry. Fat salty drops slid down her nose. Molly sniffled noisily.

Something brushed against her. A presence!

There was someone right next to her! She was sure of it!

She didn't dare to breathe.

The thing came back, and Molly had to ask herself a question: Had she gone completely insane, or was a rat currently gnawing at her binds?

Dear Charles,

My hosts have a funny habit of sleeping curled up. I mean really curled up, in a ball: arms around their legs, face tucked into their chest, back arched. It's very impressive! But logical too: the sphere offers the largest volume for the smallest surface, so it's a skillful way of protecting oneself by exposing the absolute minimum to the outside world. That's what the drop of water or lonely mercury does to resist the air around it. It made a big impression on me as a child when I realized that the Earth must be round for a reason. The surface is a necessary evil, and we live on top of it as parasites.

A parasite is a living organism that lives off of another organism. It ensures its survival in a sustainable relationship with another being from which it derives its food, shelter, and means of transportation to spread its species. Contrary to what we tend to think, parasitism is not a form of destruction: if the parasite is too aggressive, it risks losing its own resources. Sometimes the parasite is even beneficial to its host. That's called symbiosis. The Barteria fistulosa, for example, is a tree that requires colonies of ants for its survival. The ants get rid of leaf eaters that attack the tree, and in exchange the tree offers the ants its hollow branches as shelter and its sap for food. We often mocked your theories, reducing them to a kind of perpetual struggle in which the stronger being would eat the weaker, or force them to toughen up. But symbiosis is just as much a part of evolution: it's through these phenomena of cooperation, interaction, and mutual dependence that species improve.

Man, in his arrogance, wants every resource to serve his pleasure alone. He exploits the animal world, massacres the vegetal world, plunders the mineral world . . . He exhausts the world he lives on without realizing that he's putting his own life at risk.

Your friend H.

IN THE GARDEN

NOT FAR FROM THE HUMPHREY family's vast manor, Detective Jalibert was deciding what to do.

At the first suspect movement inside the Foundation, his men had immediately gone to warn their boss. One of them took off in a hurry, and when he didn't find Jalibert at the station, had gone to his house. Jalibert didn't need to hear the story twice: he'd grabbed his warmest coat and rushed into the dark streets.

Fortunately, he had arrived in time to see the Humphrey hackney carriage leaving the Foundation. In the gleam of street-lights, he had even managed to distinguish four human-shaped shadows inside.

He had followed them.

It was a long ride, several times he had nearly lost them. The cold made it all the more unbearable. Finally, he had found them again: the hackney carriage had stopped at the end of a row of linden trees.

He approached carefully. Now that he had arrived, he didn't really know how to act. The Humphreys were an important family, a very, very rich family. The kind of family that has many influential friends, even in Parliament. The untouchable kind, in other words. Jalibert knew that his boss didn't particularly care for them, but Caravelle was even less a fan of his inferiors taking initiative and outshining him in the political sphere. If Jalibert slipped up, Caravelle would make him pay for it. So maybe he shouldn't jump straight into the wolf's den.

But the lady and the professor had been acting pretty fishy that night. Suspicious, even. That was the word, the one he would put in his report when he got back to justify the violation he was about to commit.

He had to word things cautiously, but he had to say them. Jalibert knew that this was an explosive situation. John and his lady had blood on their hands, and their delicate suede gloves didn't change anything about that.

Jalibert took a few steps, hidden in the shadow of the fir trees. His eyes quickly adapted to the darkness of that moonless night. He gave the estate a sweeping glance.

Large pathways led to the main staircase. An elegant double staircase that ended at a monumental door decorated with sculptures. The family coat of arms was carved into the pediment that hung over the door, per ancestral custom.

All around, the garden seemed deserted. Even the crows were sleeping.

But then Jalibert heard a sound. A crunch. Instinctively, he sank a bit farther into the shadow of the firs. Despite himself, his heart was racing out of his chest, he was so close to the truth . . .

For years, he had been awaiting this moment. Soon he would recover the little girl.

It wasn't a cat that had made that crunch. The shadow, surprised by its own sound, had suddenly frozen, hesitant. Someone who didn't seem to be completely in his right mind.

Jalibert started tailing him; this would be his pretext to enter the home of the untouchables. He had come to check in on Miss Humphrey and seen a prowler, so he had followed them. It was only natural. His duty.

Jalibert was determined to enter the house, even if it cost him his life. But protecting appearances could also turn out to be useful: his status as a policeman was indispensable to him. One should never underestimate the art of camouflage.

BREATHING

MANON WAS SLEEPING NOW, AND old Miss Humphrey was painstakingly recovering from her asthma attack.

So far, so good.

It was useful to have a scientist for an accomplice: a bit of chloroform for the little girl, some cortisone for her, and everyone would have a good night's sleep!

They had rolled the fat woman into the cellar. John insisted she might still be useful. Useful . . . for what? Miss Humphrey was tired of all his enigmas. She was getting impatient to return to her formerly tranquil life with all its galas and petits fours. Soon. She hoped. She crossed her fingers.

A few drops of sweat were still pearling on her forehead. She had to stop smoking. She wasn't a young girl anymore, and her lungs were ready to burst.

She knew it and she listened to John's scolding with annoyance.

Her lungs would probably be in much better shape if she weren't subjected to this constant stress! She was too old for this.

When she finally managed to slow her breathing, she whispered the question that had been burning up her brain since the beginning of the night . . .

How did he plan to get rid of the little girl?

John stopped, shocked.

"Get rid . . . of the little girl?"

The serious scientist was shaken by an enormous burst of laughter. Get rid of her? What a stupid idea!

Seeing the lady's dirty look, he rushed to add:

"This child is worth much more alive than dead! Believe me, I beg you, my darling."

No, she didn't believe him. That child was in theory the inheritor of this manor; of the Foundation; of the bank assets, the horses, her trinkets, all her possessions. She also had a right to all those famous discoveries he seemed to find so important. She didn't see how this scrawny child could be worth more than all that combined.

"A little bastard child? You're getting worked up over nothing, my darling. She'll have no legal . . ."

"No what? No right to ruin my life? Go and explain that to the pain-in-my-neck Miss Rose and her followers . . . Just imagine what they'll say: the charitable Miss Humphrey hoards her orphan niece's possessions! I'll be the laughing stock of the newspapers, the butt of the joke at charity events, a crossed-out contact in the address books of my acquaintances."

John stood up, cracked his knuckles, and headed toward the large library that loomed over his desk.

"Listen, darling . . . Do you have the slightest idea who this little girl is . . . or rather, who her mother was? No, of course, you never saw her, you never bothered to ask . . ."

"Oh, John, please, how are these family matters relevant right now? If he had wanted to introduce us to her, he wouldn't have been embarrassed! You know him as well as I do . . ."

"No, no, listen to me. For once, let me speak. Trust me, you'll want to hear this . . . This woman, your sister-in-law, even if not legally, was, pay attention . . ."

"A harlot! Not from our world!"

"You don't know how right you are . . . She was . . . how can I say this . . . she wasn't like you and me . . . Let's just say, she wasn't exactly human."

Miss Humphrey sat down almost despite herself. She stopped interrupting him: she was completely captivated.

UNDERGROUND

"THIS IS ALL QUITE CAPTIVATING, my son, quite captivating . . ."

Father Bertrand served a cup of scalding herbal tea to Lbn.

"Drink this, take your time. I don't think anyone will come bother us here." He gestured with his arm to designate the cavern they were in.

Then he noticed Giulio and went to fetch him a bowl of water.

The room was carved into the earth around the various rock formations. Each wall opened onto a kind of door, a narrow passageway that led to other chambers constructed the same way. None of them were closed. They were communal crossings.

Anyone who needed to use them was welcome. These were the underground pathways that Lbn had taken to get back to where he had caught hold of Manon. He was safe to stay with Giulio and inform the priest of what had just unfurled. He needed allies in the animal and human world, so it was good to maintain his relationships. He continued his explanation:

"I spurred the animals to revolt . . . Their living conditions were simply despicable."

"Was that the only reason?"

It was useless to lie, of course, the father wouldn't be fooled . . .

"It was also a diversion to get Manon out of there . . . That moron police officer had stationed two of his guys in front of the main entrance. Not to mention the journalists who've been haunting the grounds since the beginning of the whole affair . . . If someone starts to suspect the little girl's true nature, our peace of mind will be ruined forever."

"Your peace of mind . . ." the old priest clarified.

He stood up and went to rifle through the suitcase that was serving as his library. He needed two hands to pick up the weighty manuscript he had been working on for many long years. He added a few notes on a separate sheet of paper.

The room provided basic comfort: a bed to sleep on, a wood-burning stove for heat, a table for work. These sorts of caves sometimes served as a refuge for men who, like him, had decided to take an interest in the Dark Arts. He turned to his guest:

"But she didn't leave with you, she left with them, and they know . . . Go, my son, go find her and bring her to me, no matter the cost."

Lbn stood up and Giulio rose with him.

They didn't know where they were going, but they knew they were on the right path. A baby rat had managed to slip into the car carrying the little girl, and it had scattered pheromone-filled droplets all down the path. Urine, that is.

No doubt about it, rats really are animals of great intelligence.

AWAKENING

MANON HAD THE STRANGE IMPRESSION that she was sleeping a leaden sleep, a heavy sleep, a crushing sleep, but all her senses remained on the alert. She could have sworn she heard everything, understood everything.

She had felt the hands lift her from the ground. She had followed the car's motions. She could even have listed every hole and bump in the road they'd taken.

And yet, she couldn't lift a finger, she felt entirely glued to what was serving as a bed, crushed by the laws of gravity.

She also had the very distinct sensation that it would last forever, that she would never wake up again. Her chest felt stuck in this narrow straitjacket that didn't choke her but rendered the slightest movement unthinkable. Her limbs weighed tons, her muscles had turned to marble.

But waking up was, on the other hand, violent, a sort of lacerating lightning bolt.

My God how much she hurt! The suffering was atrocious, unbearable.

She recognized the pain tearing through her back once more, but the spreading sensation was a thousand times more intense.

It ripped through her neck and descended her lower back. Her spine seemed split in two lengthwise.

She sat up abruptly, completely awake.

She moved the muscles of her arms, hoping gradually to recover the use of her neck, her body. She was still shaking.

She tried to stand, but her feet didn't touch the ground.

Manon was floating.

She was flying.

Someone nearby applauded.

Dear Charles,

I'm in love . . . In love like a man of reason perhaps, which is to say in a completely unreasonable, extravagant, wonderful way . . . My brain and heart are boiling, everything about this incredible person excites me. Oh, how I envy your tranquil idyll with your tender cousin, the beloved Emma! My own love is resting precariously on dynamite. But what can I do?

Psyche hadn't been content with the happiness offered to her and her insatiable curiosity had turned everything upside down . . . Of course, she was mad at herself for it, but what good is it to wallow in self-reproach? Psyche took her destiny into her own hands. She took off searching for her divine husband, from temple to temple, until she reached that of Venus, the goddess of beauty, the mother of Cupid, her mother-in-law. Venus loathed Psyche. She was angry at her for making her son suffer, and she was also jealous of that mere mortal's beauty. So the goddess challenged poor Psyche with impossible tasks: she had to sort the thousands of grains in a mixed heap, but the ants came to her aid; she had to collect water from the Styx, but an eagle flew to her rescue. The final test nearly ended in disaster: Psyche was once more victim of her curiosity and opened a forbidden box that plunged her into a deep sleep, but Cupid woke her up with a kiss. The loving god was impressed by his fiancée's determination. They were granted the right to join the immortals: Psyche became a goddess and received a pair of wings to follow her husband to the sky.

Curiosity is a terrible flaw, but the desire for truth is the most marvelous quality.

Your friend H.

READING

JOHN RIFLED IN HIS POCKETS looking for a pince-nez that he then placed on the tip of his nose. Then he started rifling through his shirt, took out a key attached to a chain, and turned it in one of the locks of his library. A gentle click announced the opening of the door.

"Your brother, dearest, was connected to an extremely interesting family . . . We don't really know what to call them . . . Perhaps they are the *Homo nocturnus* old Linnaeus discovered? At the end of his correspondence, your brother calls them the 'Moth People' . . . 'Moth' as in those large grayish night butterflies . . . the ones with antennae. Look, like in this display case here . . .

Do you see? Well, dearest, these 'Moth' beings represent . . . hang on to your hat . . . or sit down, maybe . . ."

He handed a chair to the lady, who rebuffed it with a smack of her cigarette holder. All this flowery speech!

"Get on with it, John!"

"I'm getting to it, I'm getting to it . . . These Moth beings represent another branch of humanity!"

"Of humanity?"

Miss Humphrey didn't really know what to think . . . Was he pulling her leg?

"Yes, of humanity! Nothing less! Another intelligent race that lives parallel to our own. And they're not the only one!! Do you know the taxonomic system?"

The old lady nodded her head, but he was no longer looking at her, intoxicated by his own words.

"You see, it starts with kingdoms, then it branches off, and the insects are separated from the vertebrates . . . You know all this, right? Then the classes, the orders, the families, the genuses, the species, the 'races.' We belong to the animal kingdom, the vertebrate branch, the mammal class, the primate order, the hominid family, *Homo* genus, the *Homo sapiens* species, the 'wise men' in Latin, and the European 'race.' Do you follow?"

On the blackboard he sketched a number of lines meant to represent the taxonomic system. When the diagram seemed adequate, he grabbed a bit of yellow chalk and traced a new path.

"So, look, the Moth beings are halfway between the two. You see? It's a race that chose another means of survival, a race that shares some of its powers with insects, but also many of its weaknesses. A species that essentially owes its existence to the secrecy surrounding it . . ."

He paused for a moment and Miss Humphrey stared at him, wide-eyed.

"But your brother discovered their secret, and it belongs to us now! With major repercussions!! Linnaeus was a fixist: each species, created by God, had just one essence. We know today that his idea of race has no scientific foundation. There is no *Africanus* essence, no *Americanus* essence, no *Asiaticus* essence, no *Europeanus* essence, no matter what the colonizers think . . . Darwin, the 'dear Charles' your brother was always writing to, shook up the notion of species: If we all have a common ancestor, is there still an 'essence' of man? Something that fundamentally distinguishes us from the rest of the animal kingdom? Your brother's discovery answers a resounding no. There is no one humanity, but humanities, and they can reproduce among themselves . . ."

John triumphantly brandished an enormous file, bound with a sort of belt, and placed it on the desk.

"Listen, listen! Listen to this . . . These are your deceased brother's notes. They are extremely interesting. I'll read you a few juicy morsels, if you wish."

John adjusted his pince-nez. The handwriting was thin, slanted, irregular, tangled—illegible, in other words. But John, after abusing his eyes with this writing for so long, knew it by heart and deciphered it with ease. Miss Humphrey let him read to her, translate for her, in a sense.

INTUITION

GIULIO HAD MADE A POINT of walking ahead of the large pale figure as they wandered underground. He had much better intuition than that half man!

He didn't like Lbn. He didn't know how to explain why, but something told him that his intentions weren't as clearcut as he claimed. Oh, in the beginning, he'd been charmed: dogs are naturally trusting of humans. But then he had to come to understand that Lbn wanted the little girl for himself alone.

Why?

Giulio didn't know, but he intuited something fishy. Sometimes he turned his head discreetly to try to make out the expression on his companion's face. It revealed nothing. Probably because of his glasses. What a weird habit, wearing dark glasses! As if it weren't dark enough down here, in the depths of the earth.

Giulio cursed and advanced. Left, left, right. He jumped over an enormous root. Right, left, left. He encountered a family of moles. They were almost there.

He glanced behind him once more to see if the grasshopper-man had felt it too.

But there was no one there. Vanished!

Giulio was moving slowly, and his legs were five times shorter than the other guy's. Lbn couldn't have gotten lost: he had purposely ditched Giulio.

Giulio roared with rage. He bared his ferocious canines. Oh yes, he would make him pay for that. *Do you hear me? I'll make you pay for this!*

The threat resounded in a long scream that echoed through the clay passageways crisscrossing the garden of the Humphrey property.

WHO ARE YOU?

AS SOON AS THEY ARRIVED on enemy territory, Lbn hoisted himself outside and immediately climbed to the top of an immense fir tree. From up there, had a view of the entire area and could harness all of his senses.

He jumped from branch to branch with no hesitation, balancing his large skinny body ten yards off the ground. He fluttered so rapidly that in just a few minutes, he was on the roof of the manor.

It didn't take him long to locate the child: a terrible crunching sound that he alone could hear guided him toward a small skylight. He slid through it carefully.

The little girl was waking up.

He watched her stretch her entire body, lean on her forearms to release her shoulders. He watched the envelope of flesh rip between the shoulder blades, then he saw the large wings finally deploy in the night.

They were still a bit crumpled, but he could see the extraordinary patterns that adorned a soft gray background. The upper wings were decorated with a garland of pearly white arabesques. Below, two red circles speckled with black seemed to wink with each beat of the wings. As the thousands of tiny scales dried, a light powder spread through the room, and the little girl gleamed with a supernatural light in the darkness.

She sat on her makeshift bed and tried to set a foot on the ground, but her wings were already moving and the child, without realizing it, was flying.

Lbn clapped his hands together. Since the dawn of time, his people had done this in pivotal moments of existence: it was a way to ward off negative waves. This gesture had even spread to the human world.

The little girl, surprised, turned around.

"Who are you?"

The gift of telepathy had finally awoken. Things would be simpler now. Lbn reached out his hand.

"Come, little sister, don't be afraid. I'll bring you home."

Manon recognized the strange character she had met on her way to the Foundation, or rather, she recognized the voice that had infused her with so much warmth in just a few words. Of course she would follow him.

She gave him her hand.

DIARY

JOHN SAVORED HIS SUCCESS. NEVER had he been listened to with such rapt attention. Deep down, he had always known he was an excellent orator! He doled out his flourishes, calculated his pauses, measured his tone of voice. He imagined halls full of students hanging from his every word . . . With such emotion, such respect, such fear, they would venture, sometimes, to ask him a question . . .

"Can you spit it out, please?"

My God, she was vulgar! He was the commoner, but he was far less crude than Harriet Humphrey. He sighed.

"All right, listen up, dearest, these letters were not meant for us, but who cares . . . In any event, their addressee died not long after our Humphrey, so he wouldn't have gotten much use out of them. And so:

It seems the Moth people have turned hostile since my relationship with Ml was made official. I don't understand . . . These people are so profoundly good, so altruistic . . . But their gazes can't lie. One thing is certain: I am no longer welcome among the Moth people.

"Let's jump forward a few months.

Ml is pregnant and we're torn between happiness at this news and anxiety about the future . . . What will her father say? What will her people say?

"Touching, isn't it? But let's go straight to the birth, I'll spare you the pregnancy hiccups.

The child is born and she resembles her mother too much to for there to be any mistake. The child is not human. Will she have the same powers as her people?

"'The same powers as her people,' take note, my dear . . . And further on:

The council met tonight . . . What will become of us three? She tried to warn me . . . But I didn't want to believe her! How can such an advanced people subscribe to the notions of unsuitable marriage and intolerance? Unless something instinctual has put them on the alert? The laws of conservation are truly impenetrable . . .

"But don't worry, dearest, I'm not going to bore you stiff with your brother's scientific flights of fancy. Just one final passage:

Ml is with the council right now . . . She told me to leave with the little girl. Leave . . . Leave . . . Leave! And with the little girl! The look in her eyes left me no choice. For the first time, I saw panic in her gentle, red irises. Leave . . . How difficult it is!

"Heartbreaking, isn't it?"

THE DROP

HEARTBREAKING INDEED.

Standing behind the door, Molly tried to sniffle discreetly. These family tragedies were too much for her, they had always made her blubber like a baby. It was a shame, now her makeup would run . . . This adventure had already put quite a dent in her elegance! Molly's nose was running and her mind vacillated between the life-saving tissue she fiddled with in her pocket and the story of this patriarch forced to flee with his child to protect her.

Her own father had also left, but with a kick in his behind because of something to do with an empty bottle. And to tell the truth, she hadn't had many reasons to regret it.

But that little kid. Pfft . . . She couldn't help it, two more fat tears rolled down her cheek.

And another drop, from her nostril this time.

Unable to hold back any longer, Molly blew loudly into her handkerchief.

A fraction of a second later, John was pointing his revolver at her temple.

How stupid she had been, how completely stupid! She couldn't believe it and would have gladly slapped herself if her wrists hadn't been bound once more.

FLIGHT

YES, MANON WAS FLYING.

With a flap of her wings, she took the boy's hand and together they headed for the open skylight, all the way up high.

Her wings moved marvelously. They were an integral part of her body. Already the wound that had given rise to them was nothing more than a diffuse warmth, barely the memory of a burn.

She hoisted herself toward the roof. She was so light!

The moon appeared from behind a cloud. It had come to greet her. In the white light, Manon deployed her large body, now so slight, and with a leap flew into the cool wind of the night.

Lbn sat on the roof and observed her, worried.

There was no one there though. The countryside was sleeping a peaceful slumber. The fields aligned their furrows, bordered here and there with tiny hedges. Only a small river traced its dancing curve, breaking the geometry of the meadows and imposing detours on the farmers. In the distance, loomed the peaks of the vast forest. The firs, straight and packed together, looked like a sleeping people over which the sky was spreading its starry blanket. That night, nature was breathing to the slow rhythm of the dozing zephyr.

Manon had the sensation of soaring over this peaceful world, of finally resting within it.

Flying was extraordinary. Never had she felt this free, unconstrained by even the laws of gravity, liberated from the human condition, almost. She traced arabesques in the ink-black sky, tasting the sliding of the air along her body which had become a feather.

Then a light wrested her from her sweet dream.

A light that was not a reflection of the moon, nor the twinkling of a star. A feverish and menacing light: fire.

There in the manor, a flame was burning.

Armed with her wings, Manon felt stronger. She approached gently, carefully, until she could sufficiently make out the scene.

Lbn stood up. He had a mission to complete.

GIFTS

PROFESSOR HUMPHREY'S FILES ESTABLISHED A substantial, but not exhaustive, list of the marvelous gifts of this people.

The most impressive, was their talent for healing. The professor had tried, in vain, to understand how it worked. It happened through the right hand, that was the only thing he knew for sure. But the principle remained obscure . . . Was it magnetism? Probably . . . Or else a mechanical force sucking up the illness? Also possible. Perhaps they emitted a sort of universal balm? In any event, when a Moth person withdrew their hand, the wound disappeared and even seemed not to have ever existed.

The Moth people benefited from an age-old knowledge that had been inscribed in the very heart of their genetic makeup. A knowledge based on their incredible ability to live in harmony with their milieu. A knowledge that we, *Homo sapiens*, lost when we conquered the tool, then the horse. Man was consumed by the fever of domination, and now he was breaking everything in his path.

But not the Moth people, no. The professor was intent on sparing them from the same fate.

They clung firmly to their secret and Professor Humphrey had every wish to respect it. He wanted to act gradually. He wanted to bring man back into the great circle of cooperation, and not subject the Moth people to the violence of domination. He promised himself: never would a Moth person come under his scalpel.

He had come to terms with this.

John hadn't.

John found his boss's scruples perfectly ridiculous, unreasonable, even anti-scientific. What incredible progress humanity would make if he could access their secrets! John wanted to see from the inside how their marvelous anatomy functioned! He saw nothing immoral in cutting short the life of a Moth person. Just one person . . . or, rather, one child. The little girl.

Gently, gently. There was no rush. He would try to keep her alive as long as possible. Maybe he could even make her reproduce? He had so many experiments to try, so many things to discover!

It would be for the good of humanity.

Just a few of their gifts could keep him busy for years.

Telepathy alone. The Moth people were silent, but seemed to be able to communicate among themselves in a precise manner.

All these discoveries, once theorized and exploited, would sell for a fortune. He could even contact a few governments. No ideological pandering, it would go to the highest bidder!

Their ultimate gift, especially, would certainly interest a number of militaries. Soon, thanks to his research on Manon, man would fulfill his oldest dream: he would be able to fly. Man would soon have wings.

BOOK EIGHT

TO THE RESCUE

MOLLY WAS IN DANGER.

Manon had never seen a firearm in her life, but she felt with a painful clarity that the object held by the man with the pince-nez had been invented to kill. That cold piece of metal emitted something morbid and mean. Her eyes pierced reality with an uncompromising sharpness. These people were no longer the slightly strange couple who had offered her a cup of tea. They had become pitiless predators. Their lips curled behind their hypocritical smiles.

Manon now saw things through the prism of instinct, and what she saw frightened her: Molly was in danger, in danger of dying.

A hand was placed on her shoulder. The little girl turned around with a jump, nearly losing the balance entirely supported by her wings. She wasn't yet used to moving in three dimensions.

It was the young man who had sat on the balcony railing. He too had changed: he seemed much more beautiful to her than the tall skinny guy she had met in the street. He had delicate features, a square chin softened by rather high cheekbones. His hair was as fine as hers, as supple too, but was a lovely, flamboyant red. Manon shivered. The man spoke to her in his strange interior voice.

"Come, little sister, come, we have to leave . . ."

The voice was soothing, nearly impossible to contradict. But Manon risked it. Once more, her voice came out without her needing to open her mouth. She pointed.

"Molly, my friend, we have to help her."

His features tensed and a cloud passed over the boy's face.

"Impossible, come with me. Trust me."

Manon had lived the sweetest hours of her existence in Molly's company. Nothing exceptional of course, but the poetess was the first person who had shown her tenderness. In Molly's small bright home, Manon had finally understand the meaning of the word *humanity* . . . To leave Molly would be to betray herself.

Manon refused.

Lbn insisted.

"Come, little sister. There's nothing we can do. We can't intervene, these are human matters. We must not get involved. Ever."

"But Molly is my friend! She helped me, gave me food and a place to sleep . . ."

He didn't want to hear any of it. The orders were clear: he had to bring Manon home at any cost, distance her from the town and from humans as quickly as possible. A Moth being lost in nature like this was too dangerous for the community. That was what the Elders had said, and the Elders had never been wrong, ever. He sighed.

"Little sister . . . you've grown soft from being among them, like those pets who would die to save a master who scorns them. Nothing good can come from them—they only care about possession and destruction. Come now, we're going home."

But Manon wasn't listening anymore. She was about to take off flying again, when Lbn caught hold of her. He forced her to sit down and undid the collar of his shirt.

"Look, little one, look at what the humans did to me. It's because of them that I can't fly like you, like all my kin; it's because of them that I am condemned to jump from roof to roof and branch to branch. Look at this!"

He slid his left shirtsleeve down his arm. An enormous scar disfigured his shoulder. The skin had taken on fantastic folds, large bright red bulges in the distinct shape of a star.

"I was only a child; hunters shot at me. They're monsters, little girl. Forget them, come."

But Manon persisted. No, not all of them, not Molly. Molly was sweet, and soft, and colorful . . . Like her large yellow shawl that Manon now handed to the young man. She would save her. At least, she would try.

Lbn understood that she wouldn't come of her own volition . . . He grabbed her wrists and started to squeeze them. She let go of the shawl. By pressing on a precise point, he managed to regulate the beating of her heart. Soon Manon would faint. It was a rapid, efficient, and perfectly painless hold. When the little girl woke up again, the mission would be complete.

Manon wanted to resist. Something in her was simmering, something wanted to be free of that grip, wanted to cry, scream, stamp its feet . . . But she was completely powerless.

She slid into unconsciousness as though in a toboggan: her trajectory was completely outside of her control.

A final rebellious beating coursed through her chest: Molly was in danger.

STRUGGLE

MOLLY WAS IN DANGER, AND so was the kid!

Hoo boy, he couldn't leave those two alone for five minutes without something happening to them! Life really isn't so complicated: when you have a bone, you bury it, and no one bothers you about it. But humans had the gift of tangling everything up like a bag of knots.

The shawl he'd just grabbed out of the air was a perfect example! What an idea to skin a poor sheep who did nothing to you, spin its wool, dye it, and then spend nights on end repeating "knit stitch, purl stitch" like a nutcase . . . when you could just simply have hair!

Anyway, Molly and the kid were in danger, and he needed to get them out of it. Then he could teach them a lesson. I mean, come on!

Giulio analyzed the situation.

That tall bat was on the balcony hypnotizing the little girl. His legs seemed even taller from this angle. Giulio would have loved to take a bite out of his butt, hot dog! He had been thinking about it since he'd been duped in the underground labyrinth. He was salivating already.

But how to get up there?

Giulio noticed that a window was open above the balcony. So he passed through the cellar, like any self-respecting dog from the streets, and hurtled back up the three floors of the house.

The final floor was the maids' quarters: the immense corridor was flanked with small rooms where the kitchen girls or gardeners slept when the manor was full.

Luckily, it was empty this time of the year.

Giulio rapidly located the bedroom by the gust of air blowing under the door and entered the little room covered in wallpaper. He climbed onto a chair, onto a table, howled to the moon, and leapt onto the young man on the balcony.

Lbn, caught by surprise, let go of the child.

It took a fraction of a second for Giulio to find his butt and plant his sharp fangs into it.

Mmm . . . No doubt about it, vengeance is sweeter than any bone marrow.

ALONE

MANON DIDN'T HAVE MUCH TIME to act.

Giulio's intervention had been a miracle, but it wouldn't be enough.

She knew they couldn't do it alone.

With a flap of her wings, she soared. She climbed high into the sky, far above the manor, far above the tallest firs. Her wings seemed to propel her toward the moon and its vibrant light.

Giulio didn't understand.

She was fleeing? She was abandoning them, him and Molly? Like chewed-up slippers? The old watchdog was stuck on the balcony. It was impossible to go back down through the skylight on the top floor, and Giulio didn't have enough of the skinny guy's agility to climb along the gutters. He couldn't jump to the ground either: he was only on the second story, but the floors of those old aristocratic houses were at least thirteen feet tall! If you counted the stone staircase, maybe even thirty feet . . . He would have wrecked his spine or at least two of his legs. No thanks. As for going through the French door, that would mean throwing himself directly into the wolf's den.

He had counted on the girl. They were a team, weren't they?

He barked a big "woof" in reproach, letting go of the young man's pants at the same time.

Lbn, in a fraction of a second, was back on the roof. He was calling the little girl; he was also begging her to come back, to listen to him.

But Manon, focused on her plan, wasn't listening. She didn't turn around until she could see the entire valley. Then she filled her lungs with fresh night air and let out one of those terrible silent screams.

Giulio understood what was happening. His entire body froze.

Lbn also understood. His prayers doubled. He made large desperate gestures at the little girl. *No, no, don't do that!*

But Manon did it.

And soon, the animals arrived.

Ravens, starlings, owls, falcons, and crows covered the sky.

Ducks, weasels, hares, mice, shrews, and wild cats came out of the woods.

Bees, dragonflies, centipedes, ants, and firebugs invaded the grass.

All headed straight for the manor.

Dear Charles,

I'm trying to understand, I'm trying desperately to understand . . . These people possess the marvelous gift of living in harmony with their surroundings. They can communicate with the entire living world and count on their support, if needed. So why not humans? What have we done to remove ourselves so far from the circle of life? It is, I think, because our society is constructed on the myth of our superiority. We thought ourselves intelligent and labeled "beast" anything that did not possess our reason, forgetting the extraordinary foolishness of most of human history . . . "Man is a reasonable animal." What a joke! Today, I'm paying for that pride. I must flee. With Ml's help, I managed to escape from the forest. I was able to contact my loyal John, he sent me a cabriolet, it should be here any minute now. But I hope to leave the little girl with you, if you don't mind. I know how much tenderness Emma has for your charming tribe of grandchildren—perhaps she would be willing to take in the little girl for a brief period? Just until I can come up with a longterm solution, of course. I have to find a wet nurse to breastfeed her, and tell my dear Harriet that she will soon be an auntie!

Everything is muddled, the future uncertain, and tomorrow seems so far away! But maybe this experience is the perfect opportunity to reflect on where we went wrong. This fragile little girl rolled in a ball on my knees, my daughter, her daughter . . . Her life won't be easy, but it could be very enriching! This little girl could be our ambassador.

She represents a potential reconciliation.

Your friend H.

BOTHERSOME WITNESS

JOHN AND MISS HUMPHREY WERE quite annoyed to have Molly on their hands.

Not because the fat poetess posed a threat in and of herself, but this unexpected witness was ruining their plan. They would have to get rid of her, and fast, so as not to rouse the little girl's suspicions . . . Normally, this was the kind of work they delegated to their cronies. But this time they were on their own; they had to move the body.

John discreetly placed his revolver in his jacket pocket and grabbed a large piece of cotton and the bottle of chloroform from his closet. *To facilitate things,* he thought.

In fact, it only complicated them.

Because Molly, seeing them approach, tried to resist. She hopped, a completely inoffensive and even entirely useless little jump, but it unsettled John, who dropped the bottle. The bottle, of course, was glass. It shattered with a roar, sending its contents everywhere. The sensation of the cold liquid surprised Miss Humphrey so much that she let out a terrible cry. And this howl of feminine distress had the direct and immediate consequence of making Detective Jalibert appear, weapon in hand.

John, confused by what was happening, grabbed his pistol and started shooting at random.

More shots answered, then others, until Jalibert finally managed to shout "Police!" over the racket. The silence then returned, and they took stock of the damage.

The office had been turned upside down, but most importantly, there, on the chair: Molly was wounded.

Her frilly white bodice was stained with blood. Her head hung strangely. A thin dark red trickle emerged from her lips.

Within a few seconds, John registered the situation.

He rushed to the wounded woman. He pretended to take her pulse and discreetly undid the binds around her wrists. They needed to come off as good people. Getting rid of the police officer was too risky. With any luck, the fat loon wouldn't survive and wouldn't be able to contradict their version of events. And if luck wasn't enough, well, he'd have to give things a little push.

"Detective, I managed to overpower the prowler who broke into the house of this fine lady, my respectable friend and boss

Miss Humphrey. There was an entire band of them. It's lucky you arrived when you did!"

He complained loudly, feigning the most extreme irritation. Miss Humphrey, her tongue relaxed by the miles of high-society hypocrisy she was used to doling out, followed his lead without missing a beat.

"My God, even the countryside isn't safe anymore! We come here to have a bit of a rest and calm, and then the strangest adventures fall in our lap. What world are we living in, I ask you!"

But in reality, both of their minds were entirely occupied by the little girl, who was asleep in the room above. They had to keep the detective from finding her. John made the first move.

"Let's bring this wretched creature to the clinic. They'll know what to do with her. I take care of insects mainly . . . It's not really the same thing! Ha ha!"

But Jalibert wasn't laughing. He was quiet, still on the defensive, his pistol poised in his hand.

He knew these two and their tricks too well. He forced himself to smile. Better to pretend to go along with their game. If he revealed his suspicions, they would get rid of him. He was sure John was already hatching a plan.

John was pretending to try to move the towering woman, when they heard a small scratch at the window.

It was Manon.

She was pushing the window open. The wind rushed in and extinguished the candle.

She slid inside. Her friends followed.

CONNECTION

THERE WAS ONE GIFT TO which John had paid hardly any attention. A power that seemed a bit gimmicky to him amid all those marvels and promises of riches. A gift destined only to interest a few old lonely nutjobs.

It was the gift of communicating with animals. The Moth people had a unique connection with the rest of the animal world: mammals, fish, birds, insects . . . They seemed able to receive messages from and transmit messages to any other living being.

Talking to animals, big whoop!

John was a serious scientists; his work would determine the future of nations. Chatting with Fido or Fifi was clearly not among his priorities.

He regretted that as soon as he saw . . .

Ravens, starlings, owls, falcons, and crows entering through the window.

Ducks, weasels, hares, mice, shrews, and wild cats invading the room.

Bees, dragonflies, butterflies, moths, and beetles whipping up dust.

Worms, snails, centipedes, ants, and firebugs climbing the carpet.

. . . He thought to himself that perhaps . . . perhaps he could have explained to them the principle of private property. That they had absolutely no right to enter his home. Or that they didn't have to bare their sharp fangs, that the fight was unequal, he had no claws, only trimmed nails, so it wasn't really fair play.

Perhaps he could have reasoned with them.

Halted them.

But with his back to the wall, he couldn't recoil any farther, and so when the menacing beasts continued to advance, when he felt the sweat dripping along his forehead and the urine dripping down his pants, he tried to plead with them.

The large mirror above the mantle reflected his gaze back at him.

The same gaze as 1347.

The look of an animal that knows it's doomed.

But, unlike the rat, he didn't really have time to think about it. His legs, his torso, his arms, his face were attacked by a thousand legs, teeth, tongues, and jaws. His vision darkened. A piece of calf was ripped off and something entered his nose. Harriet's scream rang out for an instant, and then the world went quiet.

DYING

THEY SAY OUR LIVES FLASH before us as we die. Nonsense. Molly had only seen a few select moments, and bad ones, at that.

For example, the peak of irony: it had started with her birth. As you die, there you go, you relive the pain of breathing for the first time. What a joke. We suffer like a dog to use our lungs for the first time, and we're reminded of it at the exact moment when we can no longer use them because they're pierced, shredded, turned to pâté by a pistol shot.

Molly also recalled her marriage. Yes, yes, she had been married! Well, it was for show, let's not exaggerate. It was for the carnival, when she was young. She had been elected Mother Fool and had married Father Idiot in a big ceremony. How much they had laughed! And drank too. Ouch! Her liver contracted at the memory . . . Couldn't her body just let her die in peace?

Other memories came to the surface. Just like that. With no fanfare. Things she had forgotten had meant so much to her.

Her first blouse. Discovering Villon. Her last love. Her mother's proverbs. The memory of her sister, who'd died as a baby. The February frost. And then the kid. Of course.

The kid, she had been the ray of light in Molly's final days. Absolutely. Such a sweet and cute little youngster.

She replayed the scene at the Foundation when the suit-wearer had taken the girl. She should have jumped on him, bit him.

Manon . . .

How she would have liked to see her one last time.

Was her final wish being fulfilled, or was she already delirious? On the precipice of death, she had the feeling that the kid was there right next to her, so close.

She felt the little girl's hand on her wound, and suddenly she felt much, much better. The pain seemed magnetized by the child's hand and slowly left her body.

That immobile caress gently brought her back to life.

Jalibert, eyes wide, watched the miracle unfold.

THE ANGEL

WINGS! AN ANGEL! SURELY SHE was on her way to heaven.

Molly was happy. As far as surprises go, this was a pretty good one! With her insistence on playing in the street instead of going to mass, she had always been told she was going straight to hell.

Off you go, to the devil with you, do not stop at purgatory!

To tell the truth, Molly had never really believed in all that, the stories of the beyond. But now that she found herself face-to-face with an angel, she allowed herself to be lulled by those religious tales.

But the angel was telling her to wake up and shaking her like a plum tree. This angel was no fun. She felt like it was trying to pull her sleeve.

It was decided: From now on, Molly hated morons, rain, and angels. Come on! They shouldn't mess with people like this! Their job is to do good and instead this angel was jostling her awake!

She got up, declaring that she wanted to speak to the manager.

Once she came to, she was surprised to find millions of little critters at her feet. Drooling, scratching, grunting atop the clouds—how charming!

A wild boar passed by dressed in a mink coat. And then doubt crept in.

This was starting to seem more like hell.

Blood, guts, hair . . . Two vaguely human bodies emerged from the heap of animals. The silhouettes seemed familiar. Two shrews carried bits of lace, a magpie flew off with a pince-nez in its beak. The suit-wearer and his harlot of course! A family of ducks and a couple of crows were making a meal of them. One bird grabbed hold of an eye—that looked very surprised to come out of its socket—and gulped it down. Molly, nauseated, turned around and came face-to-face with a mustache.

The man took her hand and carried her unceremoniously out of the room.

"Satan? Saint Peter?"

"No, no," answered the mustache, "Detective Jalibert . . . My friends call me Albert . . ." And he winked at the little wild child with red eyes.

Together, they hurtled down the stairs and climbed into the Humphrey hackney carriage. Why not? After all, brushing up against death is exhausting.

EN ROUTE

THE CAR WAS STRUGGLING OVER the country paths, the stars were emitting their loveliest gleam, and Albert was telling his story.

After escaping Bérengère's murderers, he had wandered for several days through the forest, then returned to town. He hadn't dared fetch the little girl: How would he have fed her? He settled for getting regular updates from the convent gardener, who got updates from the maid.

Albert had to reconstruct his life.

He settled into a crate on a corner of the sidewalk and polished the shoes of passersby and occasionally repaired a nail or two. That provided him with enough food to live on. Nothing extravagant, but it was enough.

It was out of the question to go back home. Too many people were waiting for him: the police, the murderers, and perhaps also a few ghosts, images too horrible to be forgotten.

So he polished shoes as he waited to find a solution.

One of his clients slowly gained importance in the course of his days. Not because he paid more—Albert would have refused any charity—but because his conversation went beyond the simple banalities about the weather.

The man cared passionately for his garden. Whenever he left his house, he would greet his tomatoes or his peas, and then he would stop at Albert's crate to remove the traces of dirt from his morning escapades. Albert would give his shoes a quick polish, and the man would head off on his day as a model citizen.

One day, Albert told him, "Your soil is chalky . . . You need to add a bit of peat moss to make it more acidic."

A friendship was formed.

They spoke about gardening for a long time on the edge of the sidewalk. Then one day the man invited him to come inspect a diseased cherry tree. Albert nursed it back to health. They became inseparable, spending their days enjoying long discussions about the art of botany and their nights over endless games of cards.

His name was Fagard. He was an old police officer who was patiently awaiting retirement, and when he needed a trustworthy man, a total stranger, to infiltrate a band of criminals, he offered the job to his new friend. It paid well, and there was little danger involved.

Albert seized the opportunity and assumed the name Jalibert. He quickly climbed the ranks with the help of his mentor. As soon as he could, he asked to join the child protection unit. The few hours spent with the little girl during that distant icy winter had changed him forever. He had realized that a life has no meaning unless we give it one. So he had devoted himself to helping kids in danger.

And then there was the hubbub at the orphanage. He knew right away that Manon was involved, and his blood froze. He couldn't act as though everything was fine anymore. He had to get to the bottom of who that strange child was and save her.

So he started his search for Manon, the child that had been given to him, that he had abandoned. God, how angry he was at himself!

Discreetly, he wiped away a tear. He was basically a father now! He couldn't let the little girl think he was a wimp!

But the little girl had fallen asleep nestled in Molly's arms, and Molly was making googly eyes at the police officer.

She found this Jalibert-Albert simply wonderful, and bitterly regretted that her lipstick had worn off over the course of this adventure.

AMONG FAMILY

MANON, COZILY WRAPPED IN HER yellow shawl, observed what was playing out. She could read the signs of desire in the excessive batting of Molly's eyelashes and the way Jalibert furtively smoothed his mustache in response. Fortunately, instinct revealed the nice sides of life to her, too. Perhaps she might finally understand these humans? They were, after all, animals like all the others. They did what they could to hide it, but they weren't very good at it. As soon as any kind of sentiment reared its head—love, anger, desire—the veneer cracked.

Manon smiled.

She who had been absolutely alone in the world a few weeks earlier now found herself surrounded by a father, a mother, and a brother. This brother who had come to find her, who had guided her, warmed her up, who hadn't hesitated to jump through a window when he had sensed she was in danger, who at this very moment was still watching over her by her side.

Giulio.

She plunged her hand into his fragrant fur, simultaneously coarse and soft, and leaned over to give him a kiss.

Her gesture awoke the little rat who had fallen asleep in her pocket. Surprised, he poked out his sleepy snout. Manon apologized and smiled. She couldn't forget him either . . . He was alone now, she was responsible for him, she was something like his mom. Manon thought maybe she should speak to him in verse . . . She tried an alexandrine:

Won't you tell me your name, my tiny little friend?

The young rat replied with a simple hemistich:

1356.

Manon stopped smiling.

1356.

1356 because there had been a 1355 before, mere numbers for the Foundation records, and there would be a 1357 after. And others still. How many? How many this week, this month, this year? How many at this very moment? Her brothers, her sisters, their descendants, and all the related species: monkeys hooked up to machines, framed butterflies, numbered dogs . . . An entire world that had just entered her field of vision, her thoughts, her life.

Yes, it was clear, her family had grown considerably.

AMONG FAMILY, CONTINUED

1356 stirred brusquely in the bottom of her pocket. The horses had reared up, and the entire team had nearly wound up flat on their backs. Two silhouettes blocked the path. Two astonishingly complimentary shadows, like in those films that try to be funny but without much imagination and end up evoking a vague sadness instead. The two black outlines stood out in the blue of the night; one of them was plump, anchored, solid; the other, on the contrary, stretched toward the sky, immense and aerial. The boy with black glasses.

Lbn reached his hand toward the horses, who immediately stopped their strident neighing.

Jalibert, a lantern in his hand, had taken out his revolver and was pointing it at the young man. It didn't seem to bother him. He was gently caressing the mane of one of the animals.

"Little sister . . . Little sister, stand up!"

The voice, which seemed to come out of nowhere, made the police officer jump and Giulio snarl. Were there other people hiding in the shrubs? Was it an ambush? Jalibert cocked his revolver.

"Little sister, stand up, tell them there's no need for that . . ."

1356 attempted an exit, he gripped the fibers of the fabric, climbed to fresh air, smoothed his whiskers, but a new jolt flung him back down: the little girl had stood. With a slow but confident gesture, she lowered Jalibert's weapon. The voice that answered also seemed to come out of nowhere, but Jalibert and Molly knew at once that it was Manon's. They recognized it instinctively, as though they had always heard it, as though it were simply the translation into sound of the tender gaze of her large red eyes.

"Get in. We cannot leave our friends here."

"YOUR friends," the young man replied. "And it's in this very hackney carriage, which belongs to two members of London high society who were just savagely murdered, that they are in danger. But MY friend has thought of everything, he will shelter us in one of his hiding spots, underground."

The plump silhouette then advanced into the lantern light and Jalibert let out a gasp.

"Father Bertrand, of course."

"Of course," replied Father Bertrand.

He turned toward Manon and handed her a suitcase. He had passed by the manor to retrieve the documents John had kept locked in his armoire.

"I set fire to the place on my way out, to erase any trace. No need for the world to know our animal friends were involved . . . Better to make it look like a simple accident."

Lbn flashed a small smile, as if to say, *MY friend thinks of everything*, but the friend in question wasn't paying attention and continued:

"I knew your father well, little one, and his dear friend Darwin. Preciously guard their correspondence, and come with me. You will hide within this network of caves constructed by my predecessors. No one will find you there. Neither men nor Moths. Your friends can come if they like. We will live there in peace. We will continue our studies in solitude, and one day you will know who you are. For it's not only a scientific epic contained in these letters, but your history and that of your parents."

Jalibert felt a pang at the idea that his role as father might be taken away so soon, but he put away his weapon. Deep down, he had always known, he had felt immediately that Father Bertrand was the one who held the keys to the mystery . . . With him, the little girl would be safe. He said that to her. He also told her about the priest's exquisite jams, and Molly added:

"Has a sweet tooth, he's telling the truth."

It was her mother who had told her that.

But Manon didn't seem ready to leave.

Was this really what she wanted?

Security?

1356 finally managed to extract himself from her pocket and slid down her shoulder. She felt the little claws cling onto her shawl; his whiskers tickled her ear, her neck. She let out a small nervous laugh, maybe a happy laugh.

"Can we call you Guili?"

The animal frolicked about by way of agreement, then took off again sniffing around for a few scraps and a quiet place to nibble on them.

In the end, he—like her—had a rather simple life. But could she settle now for lectures and toast when, at the Institute, everything would begin again? When 1357 would have to choose between red and green?

She had been lucky enough to receive not a number, but a name. And what a name . . . She knew who she was. She was Manon. The one with the power to say no.

So, no.

She smiled at her friends and took the reins again. After all, this hackney carriage was hers, the rich heiress of the Humphrey family. Why should she have to hide? How on earth could anyone think that she had something to do with what had happened to her aunt and the Foundation's secretary? They weren't really going to bother with a poor orphan girl like her . . . Manon adjusted the yellow shawl to hide her young wings and set course for London. For the Foundation. Her Foundation. The one her father had left to her.

She just had to teach herself to speak. Move her lips as she evoked her ideas, it couldn't be that complicated . . . She tried:

"Are you coming?"

Of course, Lbn and Father Bertrand were welcome. The reverend was the best suited to take charge of the Foundation's research. Lbn could supervise and make sure his people were not placed in any danger. Jalibert would know what to say to bamboozle that imbecile Caravelle, it would be easy. But for the most difficult task, she was counting on Molly. She was going to need all the poetess's talent and tenderness to finally make those two words shining on the Foundation marquee come together in harmony.

Those words that mankind's pride had nearly separated.

Those words that she would try to reconcile.

Science and conscience.

EPILOGUE

CHRISTMAS

CONSCIENCE, CONSCIENCE . . . Seriously? It would soon be a year since they had settled into the Foundation, and, frankly, Giulio had been more than accommodating. Without saying a word, he had endured the gang of psychopath cats that Molly had gradually brought onto the grounds, on the pretext that those poor kitties were living in the street—although isn't that the very principle of an "alley cat"? But he had let her do it. Then there was the shampooing! Twice now, he had been caught by surprise and thrown into a large tub of water. During those weeks, he'd had to rub himself against the garbage to get rid of that horrible honeysuckle smell. The year had not been easy. But now *THIS*!

Giulio tried his best not to look at himself in the glass walls of the Foundation, but his body betrayed him, and he felt the shivers of humiliation again.

THIS!

A sweater.

With hearts all over it.

Knit by Molly.

The shame.

He tried to distract his gaze with the fir tree. 1356 was scampering up it gaily, jumping from branch to branch and making the flames from the lit candles tremble in his wake.

Even the lights seemed to be mocking him. Maybe if he immolated himself by fire, he could salvage some of his dignity? Perhaps. But that would probably hurt, even so. And it would probably ruin the party. The little girl seemed so happy! She had just found a present at the foot of the tree and was shaking it ecstatically. If it was porcelain, it was now in pieces. She tore off the paper, lifted a corner of the box, and took out . . .

. . . a sweater.

With hearts all over it.

Knit by Molly.

The little girl flashed her biggest smile, apparently delighted. Then Giulio remembered: humans were a very stupid species.

It all made sense.

The mild remorse elicited by the death of the two associates. The incredible facility with which the world had accepted the story of the fire. High society's rush to welcome Manon, the miraculous child, the daughter of the beloved Professor

Humphrey, unjustly kept at a distance by her disgraceful aunt, that gold digger.

Caravelle had been definitive, and all the newspapers had followed suit: *He had always been suspicious of them.*

Clearly, humans were not very clever, and the little girl was part human too. He had to accept that. His mission was to love and protect her.

He would take care of her, swear to dog.

Molly was there too, of course. But even she, his companion, his mountain, had fallen victim to human weakness: since Jalibert had shown up, he barely recognized her anymore. Even her verses came out wonky. So, knit stitch, purl stitch, she sewed hearts.

All the Foundation employees, but also the animals still regaining their health before being released back into the wild, and perhaps all of London, were at risk of finding themselves in heart-patterned sweaters if Jalibert didn't put his foot down.

But Jalibert seemed the be the only one who didn't understand. He went back home each night with a heavy heart.

Truly, how oblivious these humans were!

It wasn't like the beanpole was any better. He came and went, appearing and disappearing at a window when he felt like it, deigning to come through the door when he was accompanied by that big know-it-all priest guy. Tonight, for the party, they had arrived loaded with gifts. Books, of course. With beautiful leather bindings that Giulio had been forbidden from chewing.

Not that he would.

He had to take care of the little girl, keep her safe. So she could preserve some of that childhood intelligence that put everyone on the same level. A profound intelligence. That of the world. And its guardians.

Giulio got up with all the dignity his knit sweater allowed and slid his wet nose over the little girl's neck. It was funny how the honeysuckle smell was different on her. She smiled at him and returned his caress, there, just behind the ear, right in his weak spot . . . He sprawled, and the scratching descended delightfully down his back.

Humans may not be clever, but they sure knew how to scratch.

Of course, he would stay. She needed him too much, she and her funny family. The woman with the hearts, the police officer–gardener, the bothersome beanpole, and the priest-sorcerer. And all the creatures who lived at the Foundation. Including the cats.

It wasn't all misery and strife, even if it was a dog's life.

ACKNOWLEDGMENTS

Manon's story has been evolving for eleven years, so of course she's crossed paths with quite a number of people, numerous impactful encounters that allowed her to complete her slow metamorphosis. I know I will forget some, and I apologize in advance. I'll retrace her biggest steps.

In 2009, Manon was a monster onto whom I spilled everything that came to my mind. Thank you to the courageous first explorers for daring to venture there and bring me back their impressions. There was Célia and Claire, future illustrator accomplices, Claire's son Mikaël, my first teen reader, Céline, Anne, and Christine, who will soon be authors themselves, Elisa with her sweet and funny sculptures, and my cousin Justine.

In 2014, I picked up her story again for Le Feuilleton des Incos. Children all over the world read my butterfly story, including students in Guipavas, Valencia, Paris, Raismes, Dubai, Serres Castet, Hagueneau, Lesgor, and Andorre. Thanks also to their teachers and to the group coordinators Alexandra and Aurore.

In 2018, there was Pow-Wow-Power. Every day I read the marvels written by my gifted friends Vincent and Marine, and I told myself that maybe I could do that too. I sent them chapters, which they read. Marine took Manon by the hand, gave her strength, helped her grow, introduced her to the wonderful publishing house that went on to adopt her. Thank you, friends!

But the list would be incomplete without Jules, my childhood spaniel, Aurel, our little rat, Clochette and Nuvola, our feline roommates, and of course Atma, who reconnected me to the animal world and taught me that the beautiful word humanity would lose its meaning if we divided up countries, races, or species.

It would also be incomplete without my faithful allies during all these years, those who followed the progress of this little paper girl and the doubts that accompanied her: my husband Ivan, my children Sasha, Zélie, and Lisa, my mother Colette, and my sisters Hélène, Marie, and Appoline. Thank you from the bottom of my heart.

Finally, in 2020, a marvelous house in Rouergue came to the rescue. Olivier, Anne-Soazig, Charlotte, and Patrick gave Manon her definitive form, the one that allowed her to fly through the world.

I hope that she will have new encounters that are just as numerous and impactful, that she will find readers to land on like flowers. That's my hope, but it's out of my hands now: moths do what they like.

ABOUT THE AUTHOR

Alice Brière-Haquet was a cherry picker and a high school teacher before she turned to writing books. The cherries have blossomed, the students have grown up, and about a hundred of her books are now scattered throughout people's homes, even throughout the world thanks to numerous translations. She saw some of the world herself before returning to Normandy, France, with her cello and her family.

ABOUT THE TRANSLATOR

Emma Ramadan translates books of all genres from French. She is the recipient of the PEN Translation Prize, the Albertine Prize, an NEA Fellowship, and a Fulbright for her work. Her recent translations include Abdellah Taïa's *A Country for Dying*, Kamel Daoud's *Zabor, or the Psalms*, and Anne Garréta's *In Concrete*.

SOME NOTES ON THIS BOOK'S PRODUCTION

The art for the jacket and case was created by Allissa Chan. The text was set by Westchester Publishing Services in Danbury, CT, using Filosofia, a revival of Bodoni designed by Zuzana Licko and released by Emigre Fonts in 1996. The display was set in Mostra Nuova, a type designed by Mark Simonson for Adobe in 2009 and based on a style of lettering seen on Italian Art Deco posters and advertising in the 1930s. The book was printed on FSC™-certified 78gsm Yunshidai Ivory woodfree paper and bound in China.

Production was supervised by Freesia Blizard
Book jacket and case designed by
Allissa Chan and Richard Oriolo
Book interiors designed by Richard Oriolo
Edited by Nick Thomas
Editorial Assistant: Irene Vázquez